D0521962

Twilight Land

→ LOOKING GLASS LIBRARY ←

Twilight Land

→ By Howard Pyle ←

*With an introduction
by N. D. Wilson*

Random House New York

Introduction copyright © 2010 by N. D. Wilson

All rights reserved. Published in the United States by Random House Children's Books,
a division of Random House, Inc., New York. Originally published in 1894
by Harper & Brothers Publishers.

Random House and the colophon are registered trademarks of Random House, Inc.

Visit us on the Web! www.randomhouse.com/kids

Educators and librarians, for a variety of teaching tools, visit us at
www.randomhouse.com/teachers

Library of Congress Cataloging-in-Publication Data
Pyle, Howard, 1853–1911.
Twilight land / by Howard Pyle ; introduction by N. D. Wilson.
p. cm. — (Looking Glass Library ; 3)
Summary: The storyteller finds himself in Twilight Land at the Inn of the Sign of Mother
Goose where well-known characters from fairyland are gathered and each one tells a story.
ISBN 978-0-375-86337-0 (trade) — ISBN 978-0-375-96337-7 (lib. bdg.) —
ISBN 978-0-375-89499-2 (e-book)
1. Fairy tales. [1. Fairy tales.] I. Wilson, Nathan D. II. Title.
PZ8.P991Tw 2010
[Fic]—dc22
2009000577

Printed in the United States of America
10 9 8 7 6 5 4 3 2 1

First Random House Edition

To my daughter
Phoebe:
this book is inscribed
as her very own
by her father.

CONTENTS

INTRODUCTION

If St. George and Sinbad settled in to swap stories beside a roaring fire, would you want to eavesdrop? What if those two heroes were not alone? What if they were joined by Ali Baba and Cinderella and Fortunatus and Aladdin and a whole assemblage of characters sprung to life from the myths and legends of the world, and each had a tale to tell? What would you give to be there?

Me? I'd give that magic stool I stole from the wizard and the solid piece of good luck I found in the desert and the mystical blade I used to kill the sorceress and her sister. And more.

Fairy tales and fantasies are as old as the world. This is an easy thing to forget. It is easy to see only the stories we tell today—fresh and shiny—and then assume that they came from nowhere, that they have no ancestors, and no narrative parents whatsoever. But today's fantasies are built on a rich, imaginative heritage, a global heritage. As long as there has been language, there have been stories. And as far back as we can trace, those stories have been about dragons and magic and sacrifices, fools and wise men and wizards, fate and luck and love. What we call realism in storytelling is a relatively new concept. It is the sapling in the wood surrounded by towering moss-covered giants as old as history, giants grown up out of myths and legends. Fantasy.

When I was young, Howard Pyle could grab me with a story as few other authors could. At the time, I did not know how important he was to American art and illustration. I did not know when he'd lived or died. I only knew that his stories were rich, that they had a depth and texture to them that made me feel connected to history and this mysterious world where we all live. Pyle knew his stories were built on older tales. He loved them for it, and I loved him for it.

Nowhere is he more open about his stories' roots and inspiration than in *Twilight Land*. His many narrators, all gathered at the Inn of the Sign of Mother Goose, are his handpicked favorites from around the world. And they each tell tales of their own particular flavor.

Twilight Land is a playful assortment of adventures. It is layered. Narration within narration, fantasy within fantasy, all filtered through Pyle's own clever and folksy American voice. Genies and beggars and woodcutters. Princesses who inspire and princesses who bewitch. Kings and wizards, quests and betrayals and misunderstandings. Pyle climbs inside characters who have captured imaginations through centuries, and he lets them speak. He lets them laugh and cheer each other on as they listen and wait their turns, as they revel in Story.

Find a chair. Scoot closer to this rowdy group and listen from the shadows. It won't cost you anything. Not even that feathered cap you took from the demon bird. Join in. Read. Lose yourself in the Twilight Land.

N. D. Wilson
Author of *100 Cupboards*

I FOUND myself in Twilight Land. How I ever got there I cannot tell, but there I was in Twilight Land.

What is Twilight Land? It is a wonderful, wonderful place where no sun shines to scorch your back as you jog along the way, where no rain falls to make the road muddy and hard to travel, where no wind blows the dust into your eyes or the chill into your marrow. Where all is sweet and quiet and ready to go to bed.

Where is Twilight Land? Ah! that I cannot tell you. You will either have to ask your mother or find it for yourself.

There I was in Twilight Land. The birds were singing their good-night song, and the little frogs were piping "peet, peet." The sky overhead was full of still brightness, and the moon in the east hung in the purple gray like a great bubble as yellow as gold. All the air was full of the smell of growing things. The high-road was gray, and the trees were dark.

I drifted along the road as a soap-bubble floats before the wind, or as a body floats in a dream. I floated along and I floated along past the trees, past the bushes, past the mill-pond, past the mill where the old miller stood at the door looking at me.

I floated on, and there was the Inn, and it was the Sign of Mother Goose.

The sign hung on a pole, and on it was painted a picture of Mother Goose with her gray gander.

It was to the Inn I wished to come.

I floated on, and I would have floated past the Inn, and perhaps have gotten into the Land of Never-Come-Back-Again, only I caught at the branch of an apple tree, and so I stopped myself, though the apple blossoms came falling down like pink and white snowflakes.

The earth and the air and the sky were all still, just as it is at twilight, and I heard them laughing and talking in the tap-room of the Inn of the Sign of Mother Goose—the clinking of glasses, and the rattling and clatter of knives and forks and plates and dishes. That was where I wished to go.

So in I went. Mother Goose herself opened the door, and there I was.

The room was all full of twilight; but there they sat, every one of them. I did not count them, but there were ever so many: Aladdin, and Ali Baba, and Fortunatus, and Jack-the-Giant-Killer, and Dr. Faustus, and Bidpai, and Cinderella, and Patient Grizzle, and the Soldier who cheated the Devil, and St. George, and Hans in Luck, who traded and traded his lump of gold until he had only an empty churn to show for it; and there was Sindbad the Sailor, and the Tailor who killed seven flies at a blow, and the Fisherman who fished up the Genie, and the Lad who fiddled for the Devil in the bramble-bush, and the Blacksmith who made Death sit in his apple tree, and Boots, who always marries the Princess, whether he wants to or not—a rag-tag lot as ever you saw in your life, gathered from every place, and brought together in Twilight Land.

Each one of them was telling a story, and now it was the turn of the Soldier who cheated the Devil.

"I will tell you," said the Soldier who cheated the Devil, "a story of a friend of mine."

"Take a fresh pipe of tobacco," said St. George.

"Thank you, I will," said the Soldier who cheated the Devil.

He filled his long pipe full of tobacco, and then he tilted it upside down and sucked in the light of the candle.

Puff! puff! puff! and a cloud of smoke went up about his head, so that you could just see his red nose shining through it, and his bright eyes twinkling in the midst of the smoke-wreath, like two stars through a thin cloud on a summer night.

"I'll tell you," said the Soldier who cheated the Devil, "the story of a friend of mine. 'Tis every word of it just as true as that I myself cheated the Devil."

He took a drink from his mug of beer, and then he began.

"'Tis called," said he—

THE STOOL OF FORTUNE

Once upon a time there came a soldier marching along the road, kicking up a little cloud of dust at each step—as strapping and merry and bright-eyed a fellow as you would wish to see on a summer day. Tramp! tramp! tramp! he marched, whistling as he jogged along, though he carried a heavy musket over his shoulder and though the sun shone hot and strong and there was never a tree in sight to give him a bit of shelter. At last he came in sight of the King's Town and to a great field of stocks and stones, and there sat a little old man as withered and brown as a dead leaf, and clad all in scarlet from head to foot.

"Ho! soldier," said he, "are you a good shot?"

"Aye," said the soldier, "that is my trade."

"Would you like to earn a dollar by shooting off your musket for me?"

"Aye," said the soldier, "that is my trade also."

"Very well, then," said the little man in red, "here is a silver button to drop into your gun instead of a bullet. Wait you here, and about sunset there will come a great black bird flying. In one claw it carries a feather cap and in the other a round stone. Shoot me the silver button at that bird, and if your aim is good it will drop the feather cap and the pebble. Bring them to me to the great town-gate and I will pay you a dollar for your trouble."

"Very well," said the soldier, "shooting my gun is a job that fits me like an old coat." So, down he sat and the old man went his way.

Well, there he sat and sat and sat and sat until the sun touched the rim of the ground, and then, just as the old man said, there came flying a great black bird as silent as night. The soldier did not tarry to look or to think. As the bird flew by up came the gun to his shoulder, squint went his eye along the barrel—Puff! Bang!—

I vow and declare that if the shot he fired had cracked the sky he could not have been more frightened. The great black bird gave a yell so terrible that it curdled the very blood in his veins and made his hair stand upon end. Away it flew like a flash—a bird no longer, but a great, black demon, smoking and smelling most horribly of brimstone, and when the soldier gathered his wits, there lay the feather cap and a little, round, black stone upon the ground.

"Well," said the soldier, "it is little wonder that the old man had no liking to shoot at such game as that." And thereupon he popped the feather cap into one pocket and the round stone into another, and shouldering his musket marched away until he reached the town-gate, and there was the old man waiting for him.

"Did you shoot the bird?" said he.

"I did," said the soldier.

"And did you get the cap and the round stone?"

"I did."

"Then here is your dollar."

"Wait a bit," said the soldier, "I shot greater game that time than I bargained for, and so it's ten dollars and not one you shall pay me before you lay finger upon the feather cap and the little stone."

"Very well," said the old man, "here are ten dollars."

"Ho! ho!" thought the soldier, "is that the way the wind blows?"—"Did I say ten dollars?" said he; "'Twas a hundred dollars I meant."

At that the old man frowned until his eyes shone green. "Very well," said he, "if it is a hundred dollars you want, you will have to come home with me, for I have not so much with me." Thereupon he entered the town with the soldier at his heels.

Up one street he went and down another, until at last he came to a great, black, ancient, ramshackle house; and that was where he lived. In he walked without so much as a rap at the door, and so led the way to a great room with furnaces and books and bottles and jars and dust and cobwebs, and three grinning skulls upon the mantelpiece, each with a candle stuck atop of it, and there he left the soldier while he went to get the hundred dollars.

The soldier sat him down upon a three-legged stool in the corner and began staring about him; and he liked the looks of the place as little as any he had seen in all of his life, for it smelled musty and dusty, it did: the three skulls grinned at him, and he began to think that the little old man was no better than he should be. "I wish," said he, at last, "that instead of being here I might be well out of my scrape and in a safe place."

Now the little old man in scarlet was a great magician, and there was little or nothing in that house that had not some magic about it, and of all things the three-legged stool had been conjured the most.

"I wish that instead of being here I might be well out of my scrape, and in a safe place." That was what the soldier said; and hardly had the words left his lips when—whisk! whir!—

away flew the stool through the window, so suddenly that the soldier had only just time enough to grip it tight by the legs to save himself from falling. Whir! whiz!—away it flew like a bullet. Up and up it went—so high in the air that the earth below looked like a black blanket spread out in the night; and then down it came again, with the soldier still gripping tight to the legs, until at last it settled as light as a feather upon a balcony of the king's palace; and when the soldier caught his wind again he found himself without a hat, and with hardly any wits in his head.

There he sat upon the stool for a long time without daring to move, for he did not know what might happen to him next. There he sat and sat, and by-and-by his ears got cold in the night air, and then he noticed for the first time that he had lost his head gear, and bethought himself of the feather cap in his pocket. So out he drew it and clapped it upon his head, and then—lo and behold!—he found he had become as invisible as thin air—not a shred or a hair of him could be seen. "Well!" said he, "here is another wonder, but I am safe now at any rate." And up he got to find some place not so cool as where he sat.

He stepped in at an open window, and there he found himself in a beautiful room, hung with cloth of silver and blue, and with chairs and tables of white and gold; dozens and scores of waxlights shone like so many stars, and lit every crack and cranny as bright as day, and there at one end of the room upon a couch, with her eyelids closed and fast asleep, lay the prettiest princess that ever the sun shone upon. The soldier stood and looked and looked at her, and looked and looked at her, until his heart melted within him like soft butter, and then he kissed her.

"Who is that?" said the princess, starting up, wide-awake, but not a soul could she see, because the soldier had the feather cap upon his head.

"Who is that?" said she again; and then the soldier answered, but without taking the feather cap from his head.

"It is I," said he, "and I am King of the Wind, and ten times greater than the greatest of kings here below. One day I saw you walking in your garden and fell in love with you, and now I have come to ask you if you will marry me and be my wife?"

"But how can I marry you?" said the princess, "without seeing you?"

"You shall see me," said the soldier, "all in good time. Three days from now I will come again, and will show myself to you, but just now it cannot be. But if I come, will you marry me?"

"Yes I will," said the princess, "for I like the way you talk— that I do!"

Thereupon the soldier kissed her and said good-bye, and then stepped out of the window as he had stepped in. He sat him down upon his three-legged stool. "I wish," said he, "to be carried to such and such a tavern." For he had been in that town before, and knew the places where good living was to be had.

Whir! whiz! Away flew the stool as high and higher than it had flown before, and then down it came again, and down and down until it lit as light as a feather in the street before the tavern door. The soldier tucked his feather cap in his pocket, and the three-legged stool under his arm, and in he went and ordered a pot of beer and some white bread and cheese.

Meantime, at the king's palace was such a gossiping and such a hubbub as had not been heard there for many a day; for the pretty princess was not slow in telling how the invisible King of the Wind had come and asked her to marry him; and some said it was true and some said it was not true, and everybody wondered and talked, and told their own notions of the matter. But all agreed that three days would show whether what had been told was true or no.

As for the soldier, he knew no more how to do what he had promised to do than my grandmother's cat; for where was he to get clothes fine enough for the King of the Wind to wear? So there he sat on his three-legged stool thinking and thinking, and if he had known all that I know he would not have given two turns of his wit upon it. "I wish," said he, at last—"I wish that this stool could help me now as well as it can carry me through the sky. I wish," said he, "that I had a suit of clothes such as the King of the Wind might really wear."

The wonders of the three-legged stool were wonders indeed!

Hardly had the words left the soldier's lips when down came something tumbling about his ears from up in the air; and what should it be but just such a suit of clothes as he had in his mind—all crusted over with gold and silver and jewels.

"Well," said the soldier, as soon as he had got over his wonder again, "I would rather sit upon this stool than any I ever saw." And so would I, if I had been in his place, and had a few minutes to think of all that I wanted.

So he found out the trick of the stool, and after that wishing and having were easy enough, and by the time the three days were ended the real King of the Wind himself could not have cut a finer figure. Then down sat the soldier upon his stool, and wished himself at the king's palace. Away he flew through the air, and by-and-by there he was, just where he had been before. He put his feather cap upon his head, and stepped in through the window, and there he found the princess with her father, the king, and her mother, the queen, and all the great lords and nobles waiting for his coming; but never a stitch nor a hair did they see of him until he stood in the very midst of them all. Then he whipped the feather cap off of his head, and there he was, shining with silver and gold and glistening with jewels—such a sight as man's eyes never saw before.

"Take her," said the king, "she is yours." And the soldier looked so handsome in his fine clothes that the princess was as glad to hear those words as any she had ever listened to in all of her life.

"You shall," said the king, "be married tomorrow."

"Very well," said the soldier. "Only give me a plot of ground to build a palace upon that shall be fit for the wife of the King of the Wind to live in."

"You shall have it," said the king, "and it shall be the great parade ground back of the palace, which is so wide and long that all my army can march round and round in it without getting into its own way; and that ought to be big enough."

"Yes," said the soldier, "it is." Thereupon he put on his feather cap and disappeared from the sight of all as quickly as one might snuff out a candle.

He mounted his three-legged stool and away he flew through the air until he had come again to the tavern where he was lodging. There he sat him down and began to churn his thoughts, and the butter he made was worth the having, I can tell you. He wished for a grand palace of white marble, and then he wished for all sorts of things to fill it—the finest that could be had. Then he wished for servants in clothes of gold and silver, and then he wished for fine horses and gilded coaches. Then he wished for gardens and orchards and lawns and flower-plants and fountains, and all kinds and sorts of things, until the sweat ran down his face from hard thinking and wishing. And as he thought and wished, all the things he thought and wished for grew up like soap-bubbles from nothing at all.

Then, when day began to break, he wished himself with his fine clothes to be in the palace that his own wits had made, and away he flew through the air until he had come there safe and sound.

But when the sun rose and shone down upon the beautiful palace and all the gardens and orchards around it, the king and queen and all the court stood dumb with wonder at the sight. Then, as they stood staring, the gates opened and out came the soldier riding in his gilded coach with his servants in silver and gold marching beside him, and such a sight the daylight never looked upon before that day.

Well, the princess and the soldier were married, and if no couple had ever been happy in the world before, they were then. Nothing was heard but feasting and merrymaking, and at night all the sky was lit with fireworks. Such a wedding had never been before, and all the world was glad that it had happened.

That is, all the world but one; that one was the old man dressed in scarlet that the soldier had met when he first came to town. While all the rest were in the hubbub of rejoicing, he put on his thinking-cap, and by-and-by began to see pretty well how things lay, and that, as they say in our town, there was a fly in the milk-jug. "Ho, ho!" thought he, "so the soldier has found out all about the three-legged stool, has he? Well, I will just put a spoke into his wheel for him." And so he began to watch for his chance to do the soldier an ill turn.

Now, a week or two after the wedding, and after all the gay doings had ended, a grand hunt was declared, and the king and his new son-in-law and all the court went to it. That was just such a chance as the old magician had been waiting for; so the night before the hunting party returned he climbed the walls of the garden, and so came to the wonderful palace that the soldier had built out of nothing at all, and there stood three men keeping guard so that no one might enter.

But little that troubled the magician. He began to mutter spells and strange words, and all of a sudden he was gone, and in his place was a great black ant, for he had changed himself into an ant. In he ran through a crack of the door (and mischief has got into many a man's house through a smaller hole for the matter of that). In and out ran the ant through one room and another, and up and down and here and there, until at last in a far-away part of the magic palace he found the three-legged stool. If I had been in the soldier's place I would have chopped it up into kindling after I had gotten all that I wanted. But there it was, and in an instant the magician resumed his own shape. Down he sat him upon the stool. "I wish," said he, "that this palace and the princess and all who are within it, together with its orchards and its lawns and its gardens and everything, may be removed to such and such a country, upon the other side of the earth."

And as the stool had obeyed the soldier, so everything was done now just as the magician said.

The next morning back came the hunting party, and as they rode over the hill—lo and behold!—there lay stretched out the great parade ground in which the king's armies used to march around and around, and the land was as bare as the palm of my hand. Not a stick or a stone of the palace was left; not a leaf or a blade of the orchards or gardens was to be seen.

The soldier sat as dumb as a fish, and the king stared with eyes and mouth wide open. "Where is the palace, and where is my daughter?" said he, at last, finding words and wit.

"I do not know," said the soldier.

The king's face grew as black as thunder. "You do not know?" he said, "then you must find out. Seize the traitor!" he cried.

But that was easier said than done, for, quick as a wink, as they came to lay hold of him, the soldier whisked the feather cap from his pocket and clapped it upon his head, and then they might as well have hoped to find the south wind in winter as to find him.

But though he got safe away from that trouble he was deep enough in the dumps, you may be sure of that. Away he went, out into the wide world, leaving that town behind him. Away he went, until by-and-by he came to a great forest, and for three days he traveled on and on—he knew not whither. On the third night, as he sat beside a fire which he had built to keep him warm, he suddenly bethought himself of the little round stone which had dropped from the bird's claw, and which he still had in his pocket. "Why should it not also help me," said he, "for there must be some wonder about it." So he brought it out, and sat looking at it and looking at it, but he could make nothing of it for the life of him. Nevertheless, it might have some wishing power about it, like the magic stool. "I wish," said the soldier, "that I might get out of this scrape." That is what we have all wished many and many a time in a like case; but just now it did the soldier no more good to wish than it does good for the rest of us. "Bah!" said he, "it is nothing but a black stone after all." And then he threw it into the fire.

Puff! Bang! Away flew the embers upon every side, and back tumbled the soldier, and there in the middle of the flame stood just such a grim being as he had one time shot at with the silver button.

As for the poor soldier, he just lay flat on his back and stared with eyes like saucers, for he thought that his end had come for sure.

"What are my lord's commands?" said the being, in a voice that shook the marrow of the soldier's bones.

"Who are you?" said the soldier.

"I am the spirit of the stone," said the being. "You have heated it in the flame, and I am here. Whatever you command, I must obey."

"Say you so?" cried the soldier, scrambling to his feet. "Very well, then, just carry me to where I may find my wife and my palace again."

Without a word the spirit of the stone snatched the soldier up, and flew away with him swifter than the wind. Over forest, over field, over mountain and over valley he flew, until at last, just at the crack of day, he set him down in front of his own palace gate in the far country where the magician had transported it.

After that the soldier knew his way quickly enough. He clapped his feather cap upon his head and into the palace he went, and from one room to another, until at last he came to where the princess sat weeping and wailing, with her pretty eyes red from long crying.

Then the soldier took off his cap again, and you may guess what sounds of rejoicing followed. They sat down beside one another, and after the soldier had eaten, the princess told him all that had happened to her; how the magician had found the stool, and how he had transported the palace to this far-away land; how he came every day and begged her to marry him— which she would rather die than do.

To all this the soldier listened, and when she had ended her story he bade her to dry her tears, for, after all, the jug was only cracked, and not past mending. Then he told her that when the sorcerer came again that day she should say so and so and so and so, and that he would be by to help her with his feather cap upon his head.

After that they sat talking together as happy as two turtle-doves, until the magician's foot was heard on the stairs. And then the soldier clapped his feather cap upon his head just as the door opened.

"Snuff, snuff!" said the magician, sniffing the air, "here is a smell of Christian blood."

"Yes," said the princess, "that is so; there came a peddler today, but after all he did not stay long."

"He'd better not come again," said the magician, "or it will be the worse for him. But tell me, will you marry me?"

"No," said the princess, "I shall not marry you until you can prove yourself to be a greater man than my husband."

"Pooh!" said the magician, "that will be easy enough to prove; tell me how you would have me do so and I will do it."

"Very well," said the princess, "then let me see you change yourself into a lion. If you can do that I may perhaps believe you to be as great as my husband."

"It shall," said the magician, "be as you say." He began to mutter spells and strange words, and then all of a sudden he was gone, and in his place there stood a lion with bristling mane and flaming eyes—a sight fit of itself to kill a body with terror.

"That will do!" cried the princess, quaking and trembling at the sight, and thereupon the magician took his own shape again.

"Now," said he, "do you believe that I am as great as the poor soldier?"

"Not yet," said the princess; "I have seen how big you can make yourself, now I wish to see how little you can become. Let me see you change yourself into a mouse."

"So be it," said the magician, and began again to mutter his spells. Then all of a sudden he was gone just as he was gone before, and in his place was a little mouse sitting up and looking at the princess with a pair of eyes like glass beads.

But he did not sit there long. This was what the soldier had planned for, and all the while he had been standing by with his feather hat upon his head. Up he raised his foot, and down he set it upon the mouse.

Crunch!—that was an end of the magician.

After that all was clear sailing; the soldier hunted up the three-legged stool and down he sat upon it, and by dint of no more than just a little wishing, back flew palace and garden and all through the air again to the place whence it came.

I do not know whether the old king ever believed again that his son-in-law was the King of the Wind; anyhow, all was peace and friendliness thereafter, for when a body can sit upon a three-legged stool and wish to such good purpose as the soldier wished, a body is just as good as a king, and a good deal better, to my mind.

THE Soldier who cheated the Devil looked into his pipe; it was nearly out. He puffed and puffed and the coal glowed brighter, and fresh clouds of smoke rolled up into the air. Little Brown Betty came and refilled, from a crock of brown foaming ale, the mug that he had emptied. The Soldier who had cheated the Devil looked up at her and winked one eye.

"Now," said St. George, "it is the turn of yonder old man," and he pointed, as he spoke, with the stem of his pipe towards old Bidpai, who sat with closed eyes meditating inside of himself.

The old man opened his eyes, the whites of which were as yellow as saffron, and wrinkled his face into innumerable cracks and lines. Then he closed his eyes again—then he opened them again—then he cleared his throat and began: "There was once upon a time a man whom other men called Aben Hassen the Wise—"

"One moment," said Ali Baba; "will you not tell us what the story is about?"

Old Bidpai looked at him and stroked his long white beard. "It is," said he, "about—

THE TALISMAN OF SOLOMON

There was once upon a time a man whom other men called Aben Hassen the Wise. He had read a thousand books of magic, and knew all that the ancients or moderns had to tell of the hidden arts. The King of the Demons of the Earth, a great and hideous monster, named Zadok, was his slave, and came and went as Aben Hassen the Wise ordered, and did as he bade. After Aben Hassen learned all that it was possible for man to know, he said to himself, "Now I will take my ease and enjoy my life." So he called the Demon Zadok to him, and said to the monster, "I have read in my books that there is a treasure that was one time hidden by the ancient kings of Egypt—a treasure such as the eyes of man never saw before or since their day. Is that true?"

"It is true," said the Demon.

"Then I command thee to take me to that treasure and to show it to me," said Aben Hassen the Wise.

"It shall be done," said the Demon; and thereupon he caught up the Wise Man and transported him across mountain and valley, across land and sea, until he brought him to a country known as the "Land of the Black Isles," where the treasure of the ancient kings was hidden. The Demon showed the Magician the treasure, and it was a sight such as man had never looked upon before or since the days that the dark, ancient ones hid it. With his treasure Aben Hassen built himself palaces and gardens and paradises such as the world never saw before. He lived like an emperor, and the fame of his doings rang through all the four corners of the earth.

Now the queen of the Black Isles was the most beautiful woman in the world, but she was as cruel and wicked and cunning as she was beautiful. No man that looked upon her could help loving her; for not only was she as beautiful as a dream, but her beauty was of that sort that it bewitched a man in spite of himself.

One day the queen sent for Aben Hassen the Wise. "Tell me," said she, "is it true that men say of you that you have discovered a hidden treasure such as the world never saw before?" And she looked at Aben Hassen so that his wisdom all crumbled away like sand, and he became just as foolish as other men.

"Yes," said he, "it is true."

Aben Hassen the Wise spent all that day with the queen, and when he left the palace he was like a man drunk and dizzy with love. Moreover, he had promised to show the queen the hidden treasure the next day.

As Aben Hassen, like a man in a dream, walked towards his own house, he met an old man standing at the corner of the street. The old man had a talisman that hung dangling from a chain, and which he offered for sale. When Aben Hassen saw the talisman he knew very well what it was—that it was the famous talisman of King Solomon the Wise. If he who possessed the talisman asked it to speak, it would tell that man both what to do and what not to do.

The Wise Man bought the talisman for three pieces of silver (and wisdom has been sold for less than that many a time), and as soon as he had the talisman in his hands he hurried home with it and locked himself in a room.

"Tell me," said the Wise Man to the Talisman, "shall I marry the beautiful queen of the Black Isles?"

"Fly, while there is yet time to escape!" said the Talisman; "but go not near the queen again, for she seeks to destroy thy life."

"But tell me, O Talisman!" said the Wise Man, "what then shall I do with all that vast treasure of the kings of Egypt?"

"Fly from it while there is yet chance to escape!" said the Talisman; "but go not into the treasure-house again, for in the farther door, where thou hast not yet looked, is that which will destroy him who possesses the treasure."

"But Zadok," said Aben Hassen; "what of Zadok?"

"Fly from the monster while there is yet time to escape," said the Talisman, "and have no more to do with thy Demon, for already he is weaving a net of death and destruction about thy feet."

The Wise Man sat all that night pondering and thinking upon what the Talisman had said.

When morning came he washed and dressed himself, and called the Demon Zadok to him. "Zadok," said he, "carry me to the palace of the queen." In the twinkling of an eye the Demon transported him to the steps of the palace.

"Zadok," said the Wise Man, "give me the staff of life and death;" and the Demon brought from under his clothes a wand, one-half of which was of silver and one-half of which was of gold. The Wise Man touched the steps of the palace with the silver end of the staff. Instantly all the sound and hum of life was hushed. The thread of life was cut by the knife of silence, and in a moment all was as still as death.

"Zadok," said the Wise Man, "transport me to the treasure-house of the king of Egypt." And instantly the Demon had transported him thither. The Wise Man drew a circle upon the earth.

"No one," said he, "shall have power to enter here but the master of Zadok, the King of the Demons of the Earth.

"And now, Zadok," said he, "I command thee to transport me to India, and as far from here as thou canst." Instantly the Demon did as he was commanded; and of all the treasure that he had, the Wise Man took nothing with him but a jar of golden money and a jar of silver money. As soon as the Wise Man stood upon the ground of India, he drew from beneath his robe a little jar of glass.

"Zadok," said he, "I command thee to enter this jar."

Then the Demon knew that now his turn had come. He besought and implored the Wise Man to have mercy upon him; but it was all in vain. Then the Demon roared and bellowed till the earth shook and the sky grew dark overhead. But all was of no avail; into the jar he must go, and into the jar he went. Then the Wise Man stoppered the jar and sealed it. He wrote an inscription of warning upon it, and then he buried it in the ground.

"Now," said Aben Hassen the Wise to the Talisman of Solomon, "have I done everything that I should?"

"No," said the Talisman, "thou shouldst not have brought the jar of golden money and the jar of silver money with thee;

for that which is evil in the greatest is evil in the least. Thou fool! The treasure is cursed! Cast it all from thee while there is yet time."

"Yes, I will do that, too," said the Wise Man. So he buried in the earth the jar of gold and the jar of silver that he had brought with him, and then he stamped the mould down upon it. After that the Wise Man began his life all over again.

He bought, and he sold, and he traded, and by-and-by he became rich. Then he built himself a great house, and in the foundation he laid the jar in which the Demon was bottled.

Then he married a young and handsome wife. By-and-by the wife bore him a son, and then she died.

This son was the pride of his father's heart; but he was as vain and foolish as his father was wise, so that all men called him Aben Hassen the Fool, as they called the father Aben Hassen the Wise.

Then one day death came and called the old man, and he left his son all that belonged to him—even the Talisman of Solomon.

Young Aben Hassen the Fool had never seen so much money as now belonged to him. It seemed to him that there was nothing in the world he could not enjoy. He found friends by the dozens and scores, and everybody seemed to be very fond of him.

He asked no questions of the Talisman of Solomon, for to his mind there was no need of being both wise and rich. So he began enjoying himself with his new friends. Day and night there was feasting and drinking and singing and dancing and merrymaking and carousing; and the money that the old man had made by trading and wise living poured out like water through a sieve.

Then, one day came an end to all this junketing, and nothing remained to the young spendthrift of all the wealth that his father had left him. Then the officers of the law came down upon him and seized all that was left of the fine things, and his fair-weather friends flew away from his troubles like flies from vinegar. Then the young man began to think of the Talisman of Wisdom. For it was with him as it is with so many of us: When folly has emptied the platter, wisdom is called in to pick the bones.

"Tell me," said the young man to the Talisman of Solomon, "what shall I do, now that everything is gone?"

"Go," said the Talisman of Solomon, "and work as thy father has worked before thee. Advise with me and become prosperous and contented, but do not go dig under the cherry tree in the garden."

"Why should I not dig under the cherry tree in the garden?" said the young man; "I will see what is there, at any rate."

So he straightway took a spade and went out into the garden, where the Talisman had told him not to go. He dug and dug under the cherry tree, and by-and-by his spade struck something hard. It was a vessel of brass, and it was full of silver money. Upon the lid of the vessel were these words, engraved in the handwriting of the old man who had died:

"My son, this vessel full of silver has been brought from the treasure-house of the ancient kings of Egypt. Take this, then, that thou findest; advise with the Talisman; be wise and prosper."

"And they call that the Talisman of Wisdom," said the young man. "If I had listened to it I never would have found this treasure."

The next day he began to spend the money he had found, and his friends soon gathered around him again.

The vessel of silver money lasted a week, and then it was all gone; not a single piece was left.

Then the young man bethought himself again of the Talisman of Solomon. "What shall I do now," said he, "to save myself from ruin?"

"Earn thy bread with honest labor," said the Talisman,

"and I will teach thee how to prosper; but do not dig beneath the fig tree that stands by the fountain in the garden."

The young man did not tarry long after he heard what the Talisman had said. He seized a spade and hurried away to the fig-tree in the garden as fast as he could run. He dug and dug, and by-and-by his spade struck something hard. It was a copper vessel, and it was filled with gold money. Upon the lid of the vessel was engraved these words in the handwriting of the old man who had gone: "My son, my son," they said, "thou hast been warned once; be warned again. The gold money in this vessel has been brought from the treasure-house of the ancient kings of Egypt. Take it; be advised by the Talisman of Solomon; be wise and prosper."

"And to think that if I had listened to the Talisman, I would never have found this," said the young man.

The gold in the vessel lasted maybe for a month of jollity and merrymaking, but at the end of that time there was nothing left—not a copper farthing.

"Tell me," said the young man to the Talisman, "what shall I do now?"

"Thou fool," said the Talisman, "go sweat and toil, but do not go down into the vault beneath this house. There in the vault is a red stone built into the wall. The red stone turns upon a pivot. Behind the stone is a hollow space. As thou wouldst save thy life from peril, go not near it!"

"Hear that now," said the young man, "first, this Talisman told me not to go, and I found silver. Then it told me not to go, and I found gold; now it tells me not to go—perhaps I shall find precious stones enough for a king's ransom."

He lit a lantern and went down into the vault beneath the house. There, as the Talisman had said, was the red stone built into the wall. He pressed the stone, and it turned upon its pivot as the Talisman had said it would turn. Within was a hollow space, as the Talisman said there would be. In the hollow space there was a casket of silver. The young man snatched it up, and his hands trembled for joy.

Upon the lid of the box were these words in the father's handwriting, written in letters as red as blood: "Fool, fool! Thou hast been a fool once, thou hast been a fool twice; be not a fool for a third time. Restore this casket whence it was taken, and depart."

"I will see what is in the box, at any rate," said the young man.

He opened it. There was nothing in it but a hollow glass jar the size of an egg. The young man took the jar from the box; it was as hot as fire. He cried out and let it fall. The jar burst upon the floor with a crack of thunder; the house shook and rocked, and the dust flew about in clouds. Then all was still; and when Aben Hassen the Fool could see through the cloud of terror that enveloped him he beheld a great, tall, hideous being as black as ink, and with eyes that shone like coals of fire.

When the young man saw that terrible creature his tongue clave to the roof of his mouth, and his knees smote together with fear, for he thought that his end had now certainly come.

"Who are you?" he croaked, as soon as he could find his voice.

"I am the King of the Demons of the Earth, and my name is Zadok," answered the being. "I was once thy father's slave, and now I am thine, thou being his son. When thou speakest I must obey, and whatever thou commandest me to do that I must do."

"For instance, what can you do for me?" said the young man.

"I can do whatsoever you ask me; I can make you rich."

"You can make me rich?"

"Yes, I can make you richer than a king."

"Then make me rich as soon as you can," said Aben Hassen the Fool, "and that is all that I shall ask of you now."

"It shall be done," said the Demon; "spend all that thou

canst spend, and thou shalt always have more. Has my lord any further commands for his slave?"

"No," said the young man, "there is nothing more; you may go now."

And thereupon the Demon vanished like a flash.

"And to think," said the young man, as he came up out of the vault—"and to think that all this I should never have found if I had obeyed the Talisman."

Such riches were never seen in that land as the young man now possessed. There was no end to the treasure that poured in upon him. He lived like an emperor. He built a palace more splendid than the palace of the king. He laid out vast gardens of the most exquisite beauty, in which there were fountains as white as snow, trees of rare fruit and flowers that filled all the air with their perfume, summer houses of alabaster and ebony.

Every one who visited him was received like a prince, entertained like a king, given a present fit for an emperor, and sent away happy. The fame of all these things went out through all the land, and every one talked of him and the magnificence that surrounded him.

It came at last to the ears of the king himself, and one day he said to his minister, "Let us go and see with our own eyes if all the things reported of this merchant's son are true."

So the king and his minister disguised themselves as

foreign merchants, and went that evening to the palace where the young man lived. A servant dressed in clothes of gold and silver cloth stood at the door, and called to them to come in and be made welcome. He led them in, and to a chamber lit with perfumed lamps of gold. Then six servants took them in charge and led them to a bath of white marble. They were bathed in perfumed water and dried with towels of fine linen. When they came forth they were clad in clothes of cloth of silver, stiff with gold and jewels. Then twelve servants led them through a vast and splendid hall to a banqueting-room.

When they entered they were deafened with the noise of carousing and merrymaking.

Aben Hassen the Fool sat at the head of the table upon a throne of gold, with a canopy of gold above his head. When he saw the king and the minister enter, he beckoned to them to come and sit beside him. He showed them special favor because they were strangers, and special servants waited upon them.

The king and his minister had never seen anything like what they then saw. They could hardly believe it was not all magic and enchantment. At the end of the feast each of the guests was given a present of great value, and was sent away rejoicing. The king received a pearl as big as a marble; the minister a cup of wrought gold.

The next morning the king and the prime-minister were talking over what they had seen. "Sire," said the prime-minister, "I have no doubt but that the young man has discovered some vast hidden treasure. Now, according to the laws of this kingdom, the half of any treasure that is discovered shall belong to the king's treasury. If I were in your place I would send for this young man and compel him to tell me whence comes all this vast wealth."

"That is true," said the king; "I had not thought of that before. The young man shall tell me all about it."

So they sent a royal guard and brought the young man to the king's palace. When the young man saw in the king and the prime-minister his guests of the night before, whom he had thought to be only foreign merchants, he fell on his face and kissed the ground before the throne. But the king spoke to him kindly, and raised him up and sat him on the seat beside him. They talked for a while concerning different things, and then the king said at last, "Tell me, my friend, whence comes all the inestimable wealth that you must possess to allow you to live as you do?"

"Sire," said the young man, "I cannot tell you whence it comes. I can only tell you that it is given to me."

The king frowned. "You cannot tell," said he; "you must tell. It is for that that I have sent for you, and you must tell me."

Then the young man began to be frightened.

"I beseech you," said he, "do not ask me whence it comes. I cannot tell you."

Then the king's brows grew as black as thunder. "What!" cried he, "do you dare to bandy words with me? I know that you have discovered some treasure. Tell me upon the instant where it is; for the half of it, by the laws of the land, belongs to me, and I will have it."

At the king's words Aben Hassen the Fool fell on his knees. "Sire," said he, "I will tell you all the truth. There is a demon named Zadok. He is my slave, and it is he that brings me all the treasure that I enjoy." The king thought nothing else than that Aben Hassen the Fool was trying to deceive him. He laughed; he was very angry. "What," cried he, "do you amuse me by such an absurd and unbelievable tale? Now I am more than ever sure that you have discovered a treasure and that you wish to keep the knowledge of it from me, knowing, as you do, that the one-half of it by law belongs to me. Take him away!" cried he to his attendants. "Give him fifty lashes, and throw him into prison. He shall stay there and have fifty lashes every day until he tells me where his wealth is hidden."

It was done as the king said, and by-and-by Aben Hassen

the Fool lay in the prison, smarting and sore with the whipping he had had.

Then he began again to think of the Talisman of Solomon.

"Tell me," said he to the Talisman, "what shall I do now to help myself in this trouble?"

"Bear thy punishment, thou fool," said the Talisman. "Know that the king will by-and-by pardon thee and will let thee go. In the meantime bear thy punishment; perhaps it will cure thee of thy folly. Only do not call upon Zadok, the King of the Demons, in this thy trouble."

The young man smote his hand upon his head.

"What a fool I am," said he, "not to have thought to call upon Zadok before this!" Then he called aloud, "Zadok, Zadok! If thou art indeed my slave, come hither at my bidding."

In an instant there sounded a rumble as of thunder. The floor swayed and rocked beneath the young man's feet. The dust flew in clouds, and there stood Zadok as black as ink, with eyes that shone like coals of fire.

"I have come," said Zadok, "and first let me cure thy smarts, O master."

He removed the cloths from the young man's back, and rubbed the places that smarted with a cooling unguent. Instantly the pain and smarting ceased, and the merchant's son had perfect ease.

"Now," said Zadok, "what is thy bidding?"

"Tell me," said Aben Hassen the Fool, "whence comes all the wealth that you have brought me? The king has commanded me to tell him and I could not, and so he has had me beaten with fifty lashes."

"I bring the treasure," said Zadok, "from the treasure-house of the ancient kings of Egypt. That treasure I at one time discovered to your father, and he, not desiring it himself, hid it in the earth so that no one might find it."

"And where is this treasure-house, O Zadok?" said the young man.

"It is in the city of the queen of the Black Isles," said the King of the Demons; "there thy father lived in a palace of such magnificence as thou hast never dreamed of. It was I that brought him thence to this place with one vessel of gold money and one vessel of silver money."

"It was you who brought him here, did you say, Zadok? Then, tell me, can you take me from here to the city of the queen of the Black Isles, whence you brought him?"

"Yes," said Zadok, "with ease."

"Then," said the young man, "I command you to take me thither instantly, and to show me the treasure."

"I obey," said Zadok.

He stamped his foot upon the ground. In an instant the walls of the prison split asunder, and the sky was above them. The Demon leaped from the earth, carrying the young man by the girdle, and flew through the air so swiftly that the stars appeared to slide away behind them.

In a moment he set the young man again upon the ground, and Aben Hassen the Fool found himself at the end of what appeared to be a vast and splendid garden.

"We are now," said Zadok, "above the treasure-house of which I spoke. It was here that I saw thy father seal it so that no one but the master of Zadok may enter. Thou mayst go in any time it may please thee, for it is thine."

"I would enter into it now," said Aben Hassen the Fool.

"Thou shalt enter," said Zadok. He stooped, and with his finger-point he drew a circle upon the ground where they stood; then he stamped with his heel upon the circle. Instantly the earth opened, and there appeared a flight of marble steps leading downward into the earth. Zadok led the way down the steps and the young man followed. At the bottom of the steps was a door of adamant. Upon the door were these words in letters as black as ink, in the handwriting of the old man who had gone:

"Oh, fool! fool! Beware what thou doest. Within here shalt thou find death!"

There was a key of brass in the door. The King of the Demons turned the key and opened the door. The young man entered after him.

Aben Hassen the Fool found himself in a vast vaulted room, lit by the light of a single carbuncle set in the center of the dome above. In the middle of the marble floor was a great basin twenty paces broad, and filled to the brim with money such as he had found in the brazen vessel in the garden.

The young man could not believe what he saw with his own eyes. "Oh, marvel of marvels!" he cried; "little wonder you could give me boundless wealth from such a storehouse as this."

Zadok laughed. "This," said he, "is nothing; come with me."

He led him from this room to another—like it vaulted, and like it lit by a carbuncle set in the dome of the roof above. In the middle of the floor was a basin such as Aben Hassen the Fool had seen in the other room beyond; only this was filled with gold as that had been filled with silver, and the gold was like that he had found in the garden. When the young man saw this vast and amazing wealth he stood speechless and breathless with wonder. The Demon Zadok laughed. "This," said he, "is great, but it is little. Come and I will show thee a marvel indeed."

He took the young man by the hand and led him into a third room—vaulted as the other two had been, lit as they had been by a carbuncle in the roof above. But when the young man's eyes saw what was in this third room, he was like a man turned drunk with wonder. He had to lean against the wall behind him, for the sight made him dizzy.

In the middle of the room was such a basin as he had seen in the two other rooms, only it was filled with jewels—diamonds and rubies and emeralds and sapphires and precious stones of all kinds—that sparkled and blazed and flamed like a million stars. Around the wall, and facing the basin from all sides, stood six golden statues. Three of them were statues of the kings and three of them were statues of the queens who had gathered together all this vast and measureless wealth of ancient Egypt.

There was space for a seventh statue, but where it should have stood was a great arched door of adamant. The door was tight shut, and there was neither lock nor key to it. Upon the door were written these words in letters of flame:

"Behold! beyond this door is that alone which shall satisfy all thy desires."

"Tell me, Zadok," said the young man, after he had filled his soul with all the other wonders that surrounded him—"tell me what is there that lies beyond that door?"

"That I am forbidden to tell thee, O master!" said the King of the Demons of the Earth.

"Then open the door for me," said the young man, "for I cannot open it for myself, as there is neither lock nor key to it."

"That also I am forbidden to do," said Zadok.

"I wish that I knew what was there," said the young man.

The Demon laughed. "Some time," said he, "thou mayest find for thyself. Come, let us leave here and go to the palace which thy father built years ago, and which he left behind him when he quitted this place for the place in which thou knewest him."

He led the way and the young man followed; they passed through the vaulted rooms and out through the door of adamant, and Zadok locked it behind them and gave the key to the young man.

"All this is thine now," he said; "I give it to thee as I gave it to thy father. I have shown thee how to enter, and thou mayst go in whenever it pleases thee to do so."

They ascended the steps, and so reached the garden above. Then Zadok struck his heel upon the ground, and the earth closed as it had opened. He led the young man from the spot until they had come to a wide avenue that led to the palace beyond. "Here I leave thee," said the Demon, "but if ever thou hast need of me, call and I will come."

Thereupon he vanished like a flash, leaving the young man standing like one in a dream.

He saw before him a garden of such splendor and magnificence as he had never dreamed of even in his wildest fancy. There were seven fountains as clear as crystal that shot high into the air and fell back into basins of alabaster. There was a broad avenue as white as snow, and thousands of lights lit up everything as light as day. Upon either side of the avenue stood a row of slaves, clad in garments of white silk, and with jeweled turbans upon their heads. Each held a flaming torch of sandalwood. Behind the slaves stood a double row of armed men, and behind them a great crowd of other servants and attendants, dressed each as magnificently as a prince, blazing and flaming with innumerable jewels and ornaments of gold.

But of all these things the young man thought nothing and saw nothing; for at the end of the marble avenue there arose a palace, the like of which was not in the four quarters of the earth—a palace of marble and gold and carmine and ultramarine—rising into the purple starry sky, and shining in the moonlight like a vision of Paradise. The palace was illuminated from top to bottom and from end to end; the windows shone like crystal, and from it came sounds of music and rejoicing.

When the crowd that stood waiting saw the young man appear, they shouted: "Welcome! Welcome! To the master who has come again! To Aben Hassen the Fool!"

The young man walked up the avenue of marble to the palace, surrounded by the armed attendants in their dresses of jewels and gold, and preceded by dancing-girls as beautiful as houris, who danced and sung before him. He was dizzy with joy. "All—all this," he exulted, "belongs to me. And to think that if I had listened to the Talisman of Solomon I would have had none of it."

That was the way he came back to the treasure of the ancient kings of Egypt, and to the palace of enchantment that his father had quitted.

For seven months he lived a life of joy and delight, surrounded by crowds of courtiers as though he were a king, and going from pleasure to pleasure without end. Nor had he any fear of an end coming to it, for he knew that his treasure was inexhaustible. He made friends with the princes and nobles of the land. From far and wide people came to visit him, and the renown of his magnificence filled all the world. When men would praise any one they would say, "He is as rich," or as "magnificent," or as "generous, as Aben Hassen the Fool."

So for seven months he lived a life of joy and delight; then one morning he awakened and found everything changed to grief and mourning. Where the day before had been laughter, today was crying. Where the day before had been mirth, today was lamentation. All the city was shrouded in gloom, and everywhere was weeping and crying.

Seven servants stood on guard near Aben Hassen the Fool as he lay upon his couch. "What means all this sorrow?" said he to one of the servants.

Instantly all the servants began howling and beating their heads, and he to whom the young man had spoken fell down with his face in the dust, and lay there twisting and writhing like a worm.

"He has asked the question!" howled the servants—"he has asked the question!"

"Are you mad?" cried the young man. "What is the matter with you?"

At the doorway of the room stood a beautiful female servant, bearing in her hands a jeweled basin of gold, filled with rose-water, and a fine linen napkin for the young man to wash and dry his hands upon. "Tell me," said the young man, "what means all this sorrow and lamentation?"

Instantly the beautiful servant dropped the golden basin upon the stone floor, and began shrieking and tearing her clothes. "He has asked the question!" she screamed—"he has asked the question!"

The young man began to grow frightened; he arose from his couch, and with uneven steps went out into the anteroom. There he found his chamberlain waiting for him with a crowd of attendants and courtiers. "Tell me," said Aben Hassen the Fool, "why are you all so sorrowful?"

Instantly they who stood waiting began crying and tearing their clothes and beating their hands. As for the chamberlain—he was a reverend old man—his eyes sparkled with anger, and his fingers twitched as though he would have struck if he had dared. "What," he cried, "art thou not contented with all thou hast and with all that we do for thee without asking the forbidden question?"

Thereupon he tore his cap from his head and flung it upon the ground, and began beating himself violently upon the head with great outcrying.

Aben Hassen the Fool, not knowing what to think or what was to happen, ran back into the bedroom again. "I think everybody in this place has gone mad," said he. "Nevertheless, if I do not find out what it all means, I shall go mad myself."

Then he bethought himself, for the first time since he came to that land, of the Talisman of Solomon.

"Tell me, O Talisman," said he, "why all these people weep and wail so continuously?"

"Rest content," said the Talisman of Solomon, "with

49

knowing that which concerns thine own self, and seek not to find an answer that will be to thine own undoing. Be thou also further advised: do not question the Demon Zadok."

"Fool that I am," said the young man, stamping his foot; "here am I wasting all this time when, if I had but thought of Zadok at first, he would have told me all." Then he called aloud, "Zadok! Zadok! Zadok!"

Instantly the ground shook beneath his feet, the dust rose in clouds, and there stood Zadok as black as ink, and with eyes that shone like fire.

"Tell me," said the young man; "I command thee to tell me, O Zadok! Why are the people all gone mad this morning, and why do they weep and wail, and why do they go crazy when I do but ask them why they are so afflicted?"

"I will tell thee," said Zadok. "Seven-and-thirty years ago there was a queen over this land—the most beautiful that ever was seen. Thy father, who was the wisest and most cunning magician in the world, turned her into stone, and with her all the attendants in her palace. No one since that time has been permitted to enter the palace—it is forbidden for any one even to ask a question concerning it; but every year, on the day on which the queen was turned to stone, the whole land mourns with weeping and wailing. And now thou knowest all!"

"What you tell me," said the young man, "passes wonder.

But tell me further, O Zadok, is it possible for me to see this queen whom my father turned to stone?"

"Nothing is easier," said Zadok.

"Then," said the young man, "I command you to take me to where she is, so that I may see her with mine own eyes."

"I hear and obey," said the Demon.

He seized the young man by the girdle, and in an instant flew away with him to a hanging garden that lay before the queen's palace.

"Thou art the first man," said Zadok, "who has seen what thou art about to see for seven-and-thirty years. Come, I will show thee a queen, the most beautiful that the eyes of man ever looked upon."

He led the way, and the young man followed, filled with wonder and astonishment. Not a sound was to be heard, not a thing moved, but silence hung like a veil between the earth and the sky.

Following the Demon, the young man ascended a flight of steps, and so entered the vestibule of the palace. There stood guards in armor of brass and silver and gold. But they were without life—they were all of stone as white as alabaster. Thence they passed through room after room and apartment after apartment crowded with courtiers and nobles and lords in their robes of office, magnificent beyond fancying, but each silent and motionless—each a stone as white as alabaster. At last they entered an apartment in the very center of the palace. There sat seven-and-forty female attendants around a couch of purple and gold. Each of the seven-and-forty was beautiful beyond what the young man could have believed possible, and each was clad in a garment of silk as white as snow, embroidered with threads of silver and studded with glistening diamonds. But each sat silent and motionless—each was a stone as white as alabaster.

Upon the couch in the center of the apartment reclined a queen with a crown of gold upon her head. She lay there motionless, still. She was cold and dead—of stone as white as marble. The young man approached and looked into her face, and when he looked his breath became faint and his heart grew soft within him like wax in a flame of fire.

He sighed; he melted; the tears burst from his eyes and ran down his cheeks. "Zadok!" he cried—"Zadok! Zadok! What have you done to show me this wonder of beauty and love! Alas! that I have seen her; for the world is nothing to me now. O Zadok! that she were flesh and blood, instead of cold stone! Tell me, Zadok, I command you to tell me, was she once really alive as I am alive, and did my father truly turn her to stone as she lies here?"

"She was really alive as thou art alive, and he did truly transform her to this stone," said Zadok.

"And tell me," said the young man, "can she never become alive again?"

"She can become alive, and it lies with you to make her alive," said the Demon. "Listen, O master. Thy father possessed a wand, half of silver and half of gold. Whatsoever he touched with silver became converted to stone, such as thou seest all around thee here; but whatsoever, O master, he touched with the gold, it became alive, even if it were a dead stone."

"Tell me, Zadok," cried the young man; "I command you to tell me, where is that wand of silver and gold?"

"I have it with me," said Zadok.

"Then give it to me; I command you to give it to me."

"I hear and obey," said Zadok. He drew from his girdle a wand, half of gold and half of silver, as he spoke, and gave it to the young man.

"Thou mayst go now, Zadok," said the young man, trembling with eagerness.

Zadok laughed and vanished. The young man stood for a while looking down at the beautiful figure of alabaster. Then he touched the lips with the golden tip of the wand. In an instant there came a marvelous change. He saw the stone melt, and begin to grow flexible and soft. He saw it become warm, and the cheeks and lips grow red with life. Meantime a murmur had begun to rise all through the palace. It grew louder and louder—it became a shout. The figure of the queen that had been stone opened its eyes.

"Who are you?" it said.

Aben Hassen the Fool fell upon his knees. "I am he who was sent to bring you to life," he said. "My father turned you to cold stone, and I—I have brought you back to warm life again."

The queen smiled—her teeth sparkled like pearls. "If you have brought me to life, then I am yours," she said, and she kissed him upon the lips.

He grew suddenly dizzy; the world swam before his eyes.

For seven days nothing was heard in the town but rejoicing and joy. The young man lived in a golden cloud of delight. "And to think," said he, "if I had listened to that accursed Talisman of Solomon, called 'The Wise,' all this happiness, this ecstasy that is now mine, would have been lost to me."

"Tell me, beloved," said the queen, upon the morning of the seventh day—"thy father once possessed all the hidden treasure of the ancient kings of Egypt—tell me, is it now thine as it was once his?"

"Yes," said the young man, "it is now all mine as it was once all his."

"And do you really love me as you say?"

"Yes," said the young man, "and ten thousand times more than I say."

"Then, as you love me, I beg one boon of you. It is that you show me this treasure of which I have heard so much, and which we are to enjoy together."

The young man was drunk with happiness. "Thou shalt see it all," said he.

Then, for the first time, the Talisman spoke without being questioned. "Fool!" it cried; "wilt thou not be advised?"

"Be silent," said the young man. "Six times, vile thing, you would have betrayed me. Six times you would have deprived me of joys that should have been mine, and each was greater than that which went before. Shall I now listen the seventh time? Now," said he to the queen, "I will show you our treasure." He called aloud, "Zadok, Zadok, Zadok!"

Instantly the ground shook beneath their feet, the dust rose in clouds, and Zadok appeared, as black as ink, and with eyes that shone like coals of fire.

"I command you," said the young man, "to carry the queen and myself to the garden where my treasure lies hidden."

Zadok laughed aloud. "I hear thee and obey thee, master," said he.

He seized the queen and the young man by the girdle, and in an instant transported them to the garden and to the treasure-house.

"Thou art where thou commandest to be," said the Demon.

The young man immediately drew a circle upon the ground with his finger-tip. He struck his heel upon the circle. The ground opened, disclosing the steps leading downward. The young man descended the steps with the queen behind him, and behind them both came the Demon Zadok.

The young man opened the door of adamant and entered the first of the vaulted rooms.

When the queen saw the huge basin full of silver treasure, her cheeks and her forehead flushed as red as fire.

They went into the next room, and when the queen saw the basin of gold her face turned as white as ashes.

They went into the third room, and when the queen saw the basin of jewels and the six golden statues her face turned as blue as lead, and her eyes shone green like a snake's.

"Are you content?" asked the young man.

The queen looked about her. "No!" cried she, hoarsely,

pointing to the closed door that had never been opened, and whereon were engraved these words:

> *"Behold! Beyond this door is that alone*
> *which shall satisfy all thy desires."*

"No!" cried she. "What is it that lies behind yon door?"

"I do not know," said the young man.

"Then open the door, and let me see what lies within."

"I cannot open the door," said he. "How can I open the door, seeing that there is no lock nor key to it?"

"If thou dost not open the door," said the queen, "all is over between thee and me. So do as I bid thee, or leave me forever."

They had both forgotten that the Demon Zadok was there. Then the young man bethought himself of the Talisman of Solomon. "Tell me, O Talisman," said he, "how shall I open yonder door?"

"Oh, wretched one!" cried the Talisman, "oh, wretched one! Fly while there is yet time—fly, for thy doom is near! Do not push the door open, for it is not locked!"

The young man struck his head with his clenched fist. "What a fool am I!" he cried. "Will I never learn wisdom? Here have I been coming to this place seven months, and have never yet thought to try whether yonder door was locked or not!"

"Open the door!" cried the queen.

They went forward together. The young man pushed the door with his hand. It opened swiftly and silently, and they entered.

Within was a narrow room as red as blood. A flaming lamp hung from the ceiling above. The young man stood as though turned to stone, for there stood a gigantic Demon with a napkin wrapped around his loins and a scimitar in his right hand, the blade of which gleamed like lightning in the flame of the lamp. Before him lay a basket filled with sawdust.

When the queen saw what she saw she screamed in a loud voice, "Thou hast found it! Thou hast found it! Thou hast found what alone can satisfy all thy desires! Strike, O slave!"

The young man heard the Demon Zadok give a yell of laughter. He saw a whirl and a flash, and then he knew nothing.

The Demon had struck—the blade had fallen, and the head of Aben Hassen the Fool rolled into the basket of saw-dust that stood waiting for it.

"AYE, aye," said St. George, "and so it should end. For what was your Aben Hassen the Fool but a Paniem? Thus should the heads of all the like be chopped off from their shoulders. Is there not some one here to tell us a fair story about a saint?"

"For the matter of that," said the Lad who fiddled when the Devil was in the bramble-bush—"for the matter of that I know a very good story that begins about a saint and a hazelnut."

"Say you so?" said St. George. "Well, let us have it. But stay, friend, thou hast no ale in thy pot. Wilt thou not let me pay for having it filled?"

"That," said the Lad who fiddled when the Devil was in the bramble-bush, "may be as you please, Sir Knight; and, to tell the truth, I will be mightily glad for a drop to moisten my throat withal."

"But," said Fortunatus, "you have not told us what the story is to be about."

"It is," said the Lad who fiddled for the Devil in the bramble-bush, "about—

ILL-LUCK AND THE FIDDLER

Once upon a time St. Nicholas came down into the world to take a peep at the old place and see how things looked in the spring-time. On he stepped along the road to the town where he used to live, for he had a notion to find out whether things were going on nowadays as they one time did. By-and-by he came to a crossroad, and who should he see sitting there but Ill-Luck himself. Ill-Luck's face was as gray as ashes, and his hair as white as snow—for he is as old as Grandfather Adam—and two great wings grew out of his shoulders—for he flies fast and comes quickly to those whom he visits, does Ill-Luck.

Now, St. Nicholas had a pocketful of hazelnuts, which he kept cracking and eating as he trudged along the road, and just then he came upon one with a wormhole in it. When he saw

Ill-Luck it came into his head to do a good turn to poor sorrowful man.

"Good-morning, Ill-Luck," said he.

"Good-morning, St. Nicholas," said Ill-Luck.

"You look as hale and strong as ever," said St. Nicholas.

"Ah, yes," said Ill-Luck, "I find plenty to do in this world of woe."

"They tell me," said St. Nicholas, "that you can go wherever you choose, even if it be through a key-hole; now, is that so?"

"Yes," said Ill-Luck, "it is."

"Well, look now, friend," said St. Nicholas, "could you go into this hazelnut if you chose to?"

"Yes," said Ill-Luck, "I could indeed."

"I should like to see you," said St. Nicholas; "for then I should be of a mind to believe what people say of you."

"Well," said Ill-Luck, "I have not much time to be pottering and playing upon Jack's fiddle; but to oblige an old friend"— thereupon he made himself small and smaller, and—phst! he was in the nut before you could wink.

Then what do you think St. Nicholas did? In his hand he held a little plug of wood, and no sooner had Ill-Luck entered the nut than he stuck the plug in the hole, and there was man's enemy as tight as a fly in a bottle.

"So!" said St. Nicholas, "that's a piece of work well done." Then he tossed the hazelnut under the roots of an oak tree near by, and went his way.

And that is how this story begins.

Well, the hazelnut lay and lay and lay, and all the time that it lay there nobody met with ill-luck; but, one day, who should come traveling that way but a rogue of a Fiddler, with his fiddle under his arm. The day was warm, and he was tired; so down he sat under the shade of the oak tree to rest his legs. By-and-by he heard a little shrill voice piping and crying, "Let me out! Let me out! Let me out!"

The Fiddler looked up and down, but he could see nobody. "Who are you?" said he.

"I am Ill-Luck! Let me out! Let me out!"

"Let you out?" said the Fiddler. "Not I; if you are bottled up here it is the better for all of us;" and, so saying, he tucked his fiddle under his arm and off he marched.

But before he had gone six steps he stopped. He was one of your peering, prying sort, and liked more than a little to know all that was to be known about this or that or the other thing that he chanced to see or hear. "I wonder where Ill-Luck can be, to be in such a tight place as he seems to be caught in," said he to himself; and back he came again. "Where are you, Ill-Luck?" said he.

"Here I am," said Ill-Luck—"here in this hazelnut, under the roots of the oak tree."

Thereupon the Fiddler laid aside his fiddle and bow, and fell to poking and prying under the roots until he found the nut. Then he began twisting and turning it in his fingers, looking first on one side and then on the other, and all the while Ill-Luck kept crying, "Let me out! Let me out!"

It was not long before the Fiddler found the little wooden plug, and then nothing would do but he must take a peep inside the nut to see if Ill-Luck was really there. So he picked and pulled at the wooden plug, until at last out it came; and—phst! Pop! Out came Ill-Luck along with it.

Plague take the Fiddler! said I.

"Listen," said Ill-Luck. "It has been many a long day that I have been in that hazelnut, and you are the man that has let me out; for once in a way I will do a good turn to a poor human body." Therewith, and without giving the Fiddler time to speak a word, Ill-Luck caught him up by the belt, and—whiz! Away he flew like a bullet, over hill and over valley, over moor and over mountain, so fast that not enough wind was left in the Fiddler's stomach to say "Boo!"

By-and-by he came to a garden, and there he let the Fiddler drop on the soft grass below. Then away he flew to attend to other matters of greater need.

When the Fiddler had gathered his wits together, and himself to his feet, he saw that he lay in a beautiful garden of flowers and fruit trees and marble walks and what not, and that at the end of it stood a great, splendid house, all built of white marble, with a fountain in front, and peacocks strutting about on the lawn.

Well, the Fiddler smoothed down his hair and brushed his clothes a bit, and off he went to see what was to be seen at the grand house at the end of the garden.

He entered the door, and nobody said no to him. Then he passed through one room after another, and each was finer than the one he left behind. Many servants stood around; but they only bowed, and never asked whence he came.

At last he came to a room where a little old man sat at a table. The table was spread with a feast that smelled so good that it brought tears to the Fiddler's eyes and water to his mouth, and all the plates were of pure gold. The little old man sat alone, but another place was spread, as though he were expecting some one. As the Fiddler came in the little old man nodded and smiled. "Welcome!" he cried; "and have you come at last?"

"Yes," said the Fiddler, "I have. It was Ill-Luck that brought me."

"Nay," said the little old man, "do not say that. Sit down to the table and eat; and when I have told you all, you will say it was not Ill-Luck, but Good-Luck, that brought you."

The Fiddler had his own mind about that; but, all the same, down he sat at the table, and fell to with knife and fork at the good things, as though he had not had a bite to eat for a week of Sundays.

"I am the richest man in the world," said the little old man, after a while.

"I am glad to hear it," said the Fiddler.

"You may well be," said the old man, "for I am all alone in the world, and without wife or child. And this morning I said to myself that the first body that came to my house I would take for a son—or a daughter, as the case might be. You are the first, and so you shall live with me as long as I live, and after I am gone everything that I have shall be yours."

The Fiddler did nothing but stare with open eyes and mouth, as though he would never shut either again.

Well, the Fiddler lived with the old man for maybe three or four days as snug and happy a life as ever a mouse passed in a green cheese. As for the gold and silver and jewels—why, they were as plentiful in that house as dust in a mill! Everything the Fiddler wanted came to his hand. He lived high, and slept soft and warm, and never knew what it was to want either more or less, or great or small. In all of those three or four days he did nothing but enjoy himself with might and main.

But by-and-by he began to wonder where all the good things came from. Then, before long, he fell to pestering the old man with questions about the matter.

At first the old man put him off with short answers, but the Fiddler was a master-hand at finding out anything that he wanted to know. He dinned and drummed and worried until flesh and blood could stand it no longer. So at last the old man said that he would show him the treasure-house where all his wealth came from, and at that the Fiddler was tickled beyond measure.

The old man took a key from behind the door and led him out into the garden. There in a corner by the wall was a great trap-door of iron. The old man fitted the key to the lock and turned it. He lifted the door, and then went down a steep flight of stone steps, and the Fiddler followed close at his heels. Down below it was as light as day, for in the center of the room hung a great lamp that shone with a bright light and lit up all the place as bright as day. In the floor were set three great basins of marble: one was nearly full of silver, one of gold, and one of gems of all sorts.

"All this is mine," said the old man, "and after I am gone it shall be yours. It was left to me as I will leave it to you, and in the meantime you may come and go as you choose and fill your pockets whenever you wish to. But there is one thing you must not do: you must never open that door yonder at the back of the room. Should you do so, Ill-Luck will be sure to overtake you."

Oh no! The Fiddler would never think of doing such a thing as opening the door. The silver and gold and jewels were enough for him. But since the old man had given him leave, he would just help himself to a few of the fine things. So he stuffed his pockets full, and then he followed the old man up the steps and out into the sunlight again.

It took him maybe an hour to count all the money and jewels he had brought up with him. After he had done that, he began to wonder what was inside of the little door at the back of the room. First he wondered; then he began to grow curious; then he began to itch and tingle and burn as though fifty thousand I-want-to-know nettles were sticking into him from top to toe. At last he could stand it no longer. "I'll just go down yonder," said he, "and peep through the key-hole; perhaps I can see what is there without opening the door."

So down he took the key and off he marched to the garden. He opened the trap-door, and went down the steep steps to the room below. There was the door at the end of the room, but when he came to look there was no key-hole to it. "Pshaw!" said he, "here is a pretty state of affairs. Tut! tut! tut! Well, since I have come so far, it would be a pity to turn back without seeing more." So he opened the door and peeped in.

"Pooh!" said the Fiddler, "there's nothing there, after all," and he opened the door wide.

Before him was a great long passageway, and at the far end of it he could see a spark of light as though the sun were shining there. He listened, and after a while he heard a sound like the waves beating on the shore. "Well," said he, "this is the most curious thing I have seen for a long time. Since I have come so far, I may as well see the end of it." So he entered the passageway, and closed the door behind him.

He went on and on, and the spark of light kept growing larger and larger, and by-and-by—pop! out he came at the other end of the passage.

Sure enough, there he stood on the sea-shore, with the waves beating and dashing on the rocks. He stood looking and wondering to find himself in such a place, when all of a sudden something came with a whiz and a rush and caught him by the belt, and away he flew like a bullet.

By-and-by he managed to screw his head around and look

up, and there it was Ill-Luck that had him. "I thought so," said the Fiddler; and then he gave over kicking.

Well; on and on they flew, over hill and valley, over moor and mountain, until they came to another garden, and there Ill-Luck let the Fiddler drop.

Swash! Down he fell into the top of an apple tree, and there he hung in the branches.

It was the garden of a royal castle, and all had been weeping and woe (though they were beginning now to pick up their smiles again), and this was the reason why: The king of that country had died, and no one was left behind him but the queen. But she was a prize, for not only was the kingdom hers, but she was as young as a spring apple and as pretty as a picture; so that there was no end of those who would have liked to have had her, each man for his own. Even that day there were three princes at the castle, each one wanting the queen to marry him; and the wrangling and bickering and squabbling that was going on was enough to deafen a body. The poor young queen was tired to death with it all, and so she had come out into the garden for a bit of rest; and there she sat under the shade of an apple tree, fanning herself and crying, when—

Swash! Down fell the Fiddler into the apple tree and

down fell a dozen apples, popping and tumbling about the queen's ears.

The queen looked up and screamed, and the Fiddler climbed down.

"Where did you come from?" said she.

"Oh, Ill-Luck brought me," said the Fiddler.

"Nay," said the queen, "do not say so. You fell from heaven, for I saw it with my eyes and heard it with my ears. I see how it is now. You were sent hither from heaven to be my husband, and my husband you shall be. You shall be king of this country, half-and-half with me as queen, and shall sit on a throne beside me."

You can guess whether or not that was music to the Fiddler's ears.

So the princes were sent packing, and the Fiddler was married to the queen, and reigned in that country.

Well, three or four days passed, and all was as sweet and happy as a spring day. But at the end of that time the Fiddler began to wonder what was to be seen in the castle. The queen was very fond of him, and was glad enough to show him all the fine things that were to be seen; so hand in hand they went everywhere, from garret to cellar.

But you should have seen how splendid it all was! The

Fiddler felt more certain than ever that it was better to be a king than to be the richest man in the world, and he was as glad as glad could be that Ill-Luck had brought him from the rich little old man over yonder to this.

So he saw everything in the castle but one thing. "What is behind that door?" said he.

"Ah! That," said the queen, "you must not ask or wish to know. Should you open that door Ill-Luck will be sure to overtake you."

"Pooh!" said the Fiddler, "I don't care to know, anyhow," and off they went, hand in hand.

Yes, that was a very fine thing to say; but before an hour had gone by the Fiddler's head began to hum and buzz like a beehive. "I don't believe," said he, "there would be a grain of harm in my peeping inside that door; all the same, I will not do it. I will just go down and peep through the key-hole." So off he went to do as he said; but there was no key-hole to that door, either. "Why, look!" said he, "it is just like the door at the rich man's house over yonder; I wonder if it is the same inside as outside," and he opened the door and peeped in. Yes; there was the long passage and the spark of light at the far end, as though the sun were shining. He cocked his head to one side and listened. "Yes," said he, "I think I hear the water rushing, but I am not sure; I will just go a little farther in and listen," and so he entered and closed the door behind him. Well, he went on and on until—pop! there he was out at the farther end, and before he knew what he was about he had stepped out upon the sea-shore, just as he had done before.

Whiz! Whirr! Away flew the Fiddler like a bullet, and there was Ill-Luck carrying him by the belt again. Away they sped, over hill and valley, over moor and mountain, until the Fiddler's head grew so dizzy that he had to shut his eyes. Suddenly Ill-Luck let him drop, and down he fell—thump! bump!—on the hard ground. Then he opened his eyes and sat up, and, lo and behold! there he was, under the oak tree whence he had started in the first place. There lay his fiddle, just as he had left it. He picked it up and ran his fingers over the strings—thrum, twang! Then he got to his feet and brushed the dirt and grass from his knees. He tucked his fiddle under his arm, and off he stepped upon the way he had been going at first.

"Just to think!" said he, "I would either have been the richest man in the world, or else I would have been a king, if it had not been for Ill-Luck."

And that is the way we all of us talk.

DR. FAUSTUS had sat all the while neither drinking ale nor smoking tobacco, but with his hands folded, and in silence. "I know not why it is," said he, "but that story of yours, my friend, brings to my mind a story of a man whom I once knew—a great magician in his time, and a necromancer and a chemist and an alchemist and mathematician and a rhetorician, an astronomer, an astrologer, and a philosopher as well."

"'Tis a long list of excellency," said old Bidpai.

"'Tis not as long as was his head," said Dr. Faustus.

"It would be good for us all to hear a story of such a man," said old Bidpai.

"Nay," said Dr. Faustus, "the story is not altogether of the man himself, but rather of a pupil who came to learn wisdom of him."

"And the name of your story is what?" said Fortunatus.

"It hath no name," said Dr. Faustus.

"Nay," said St. George, "everything must have a name."

"It hath no name," said Dr. Faustus. "But I shall give it a name, and it shall be—

EMPTY BOTTLES

In the old, old days when men were wiser than they are in these times, there lived a great philosopher and magician, by name Nicholas Flamel. Not only did he know all the actual sciences, but the black arts as well, and magic, and what not. He conjured demons so that when a body passed the house of a moonlight night a body might see imps, great and small, little and big, sitting on the chimney stacks and the ridge-pole, clattering their heels on the tiles and chatting together.

He could change iron and lead into silver and gold; he discovered the elixir of life, and might have been living even to this day had he thought it worth while to do so.

There was a student at the university whose name was Gebhart, who was so well acquainted with algebra and geometry that he could tell at a single glance how many drops of water there were in a bottle of wine. As for Latin and Greek—he could patter them off like his A B C's. Nevertheless, he was not satisfied with the things he knew, but was for learning the things that no schools could teach him. So one day he came knocking at Nicholas Flamel's door.

"Come in," said the wise man, and there Gebhart found him sitting in the midst of his books and bottles and diagrams and dust and chemicals and cobwebs, making strange figures upon the table with jackstraws and a piece of chalk—for your true wise man can squeeze more learning out of jackstraws and a piece of chalk than we common folk can get out of all the books in the world.

No one else was in the room but the wise man's servant, whose name was Babette.

"What is it you want?" said the wise man, looking at Gebhart over the rim of his spectacles.

"Master," said Gebhart, "I have studied day after day at the university, and from early in the morning until late at night, so that my head has hummed and my eyes were sore, yet I have not learned those things that I wish most of all to know—the arts that no one but you can teach. Will you take me as your pupil?"

The wise man shook his head.

"Many would like to be as wise as that," said he, "and few there be who can become so. Now tell me. Suppose all the riches of the world were offered to you, would you rather be wise?"

"Yes."

"Suppose you might have all the rank and power of a king or of an emperor, would you rather be wise?"

"Yes."

"Suppose I undertook to teach you, would you give up everything of joy and of pleasure to follow me?"

"Yes."

"Perhaps you are hungry," said the master.

"Yes," said the student, "I am."

"Then, Babette, you may bring some bread and cheese."

It seemed to Gebhart that he had learned all that Nicholas Flamel had to teach him.

It was in the gray of the dawning, and the master took the pupil by the hand and led him up the rickety stairs to the roof of the house, where nothing was to be seen but gray sky, high roofs, and chimney stacks from which the smoke rose straight into the still air.

"Now," said the master, "I have taught you nearly all of the science that I know, and the time has come to show you the wonderful thing that has been waiting for us from the beginning when time was. You have given up wealth and the world and pleasure and joy and love for the sake of wisdom. Now, then, comes the last test—whether you can remain faithful to me to the end; if you fail in it, all is lost that you have gained."

After he had said that he stripped his cloak away from his shoulders and laid bare the skin. Then he took a bottle of red liquor and began bathing his shoulder-blades with it; and as Gebhart, squatting upon the ridge-pole, looked, he saw two little lumps bud out upon the smooth skin, and then grow and grow and grow until they became two great wings as white as snow.

"Now then," said the master, "take me by the belt and grip fast, for there is a long, long journey before us, and if you should lose your head and let go your hold you will fall and be dashed to pieces."

Then he spread the two great wings, and away he flew as fast as the wind, with Gebhart hanging to his belt.

Over hills, over dales, over mountains, over moors he flew, with the brown earth lying so far below that horses and cows looked like pismires and men like fleas.

Then, by-and-by, it was over the ocean they were crossing, with the great ships that pitched and tossed below looking like chips in a puddle in rainy weather.

At last they came to a strange land, far, far away, and there the master lit upon a sea-shore where the sand was as white as silver. As soon as his feet touched the hard ground the great wings were gone like a puff of smoke, and the wise man walked like any other body.

At the edge of the sandy beach was a great, high, naked cliff; and the only way of reaching the top was by a flight of stone steps, as slippery as glass, cut in the solid rock.

The wise man led the way, and the student followed close at his heels, every now and then slipping and stumbling so that, had it not been for the help that the master gave him, he would have fallen more than once and have been dashed to pieces upon the rocks below.

At last they reached the top, and there found themselves in a desert, without stick of wood or blade of grass, but only gray stones and skulls and bones bleaching in the sun.

In the middle of the plain was a castle such as the eyes of man never saw before, for it was built all of crystal from roof to cellar. Around it was a high wall of steel, and in the wall were seven gates of polished brass.

The wise man led the way straight to the middle gate of the seven, where there hung a horn of pure silver, which he set to his lips. He blew a blast so loud and shrill that it made Geb-hart's ears tingle. In an instant there sounded a great rumble and grumble like the noise of loud thunder, and the gates of brass swung slowly back, as though of themselves.

But when Gebhart saw what he saw within the gates his heart crumbled away for fear, and his knees knocked together; for there, in the very middle of the way, stood a monstrous, hideous dragon, that blew out flames and clouds of smoke from his gaping mouth like a chimney a-fire.

But the wise master was as cool as smooth water; he thrust his hand into the bosom of his jacket and drew forth a little black box, which he flung straight into the gaping mouth.

Snap!—the dragon swallowed the box.

The next moment it gave a great, loud, terrible cry, and, clapping and rattling its wings, leaped into the air and flew away, bellowing like a bull.

If Gebhart had been wonder-struck at seeing the outside of the castle, he was ten thousand times more amazed to see the inside thereof. For, as the master led the way and he followed, he passed through four-and-twenty rooms, each one more wonderful than the other. Everywhere was gold and silver and dazzling jewels that glistened so brightly that one had to shut one's eyes to their sparkle. Beside all this, there were silks and satins and velvets and laces and crystal and ebony and sandal-wood that smelled sweeter than musk and rose leaves. All the wealth of the world brought together into one place could not make such riches as Gebhart saw with his two eyes in these four-and-twenty rooms. His heart beat fast within him.

At last they reached a little door of solid iron, beside which hung a sword with a blade that shone like lightning. The master took the sword in one hand and laid the other upon the latch of the door. Then he turned to Gebhart and spoke for the first time since they had started upon their long journey.

"In this room," said he, "you will see a strange thing happen, and in a little while I shall be as one dead. As soon as that comes to pass, go you straightway through to the room beyond, where you will find upon a marble table a goblet of water and a silver dagger. Touch nothing else, and look at nothing else, for if you do all will be lost to both of us. Bring the water straightway, and sprinkle my face with it, and when that is done you and I will be the wisest and greatest men that ever lived, for I will make you equal to myself in all that I know. So now swear to do what I have just bid you, and not turn aside a hair's breadth in the going and the coming."

"I swear," said Gebhart, and crossed his heart.

Then the master opened the door and entered, with Gebhart close at his heels.

In the center of the room was a great red cock, with eyes that shone like sparks of fire. So soon as he saw the master he flew at him, screaming fearfully, and spitting out darts of fire that blazed and sparkled like lightning.

It was a dreadful battle between the master and the cock. Up and down they fought, and here and there. Sometimes the student could see the wise man whirling and striking with his sword; and then again he would be hidden in a sheet of flame. But after a while he made a lucky stroke, and off flew the cock's head. Then, lo and behold! Instead of a cock it was a great, hairy, demon that lay dead on the floor.

But, though the master had conquered, he looked like one sorely sick. He was just able to stagger to a couch that stood by the wall, and there he fell and lay, without breath or motion, like one dead, and as white as wax.

As soon as Gebhart had gathered his wits together he remembered what the master had said about the other room.

The door of it was also of iron. He opened it and passed within, and there saw two great tables or blocks of polished marble. Upon one was the dagger and a goblet of gold brimming with water. Upon the other lay the figure of a woman, and as Gebhart looked at her he thought her more beautiful than any thought or dream could picture. But her eyes were closed, and she lay like a lifeless figure of wax.

After Gebhart had gazed at her a long, long time, he took

up the goblet and the dagger from the table and turned towards the door.

Then, before he left that place, he thought that he would have just one more look at the beautiful figure. So he did, and gazed and gazed until his heart melted away within him like a lump of butter; and, hardly knowing what he did, he stooped and kissed the lips.

Instantly he did so a great humming sound filled the whole castle, so sweet and musical that it made him tremble to listen. Then suddenly the figure opened its eyes and looked straight at him.

"At last!" she said; "have you come at last?"

"Yes," said Gebhart, "I have come."

Then the beautiful woman arose and stepped down from the table to the floor; and if Gebhart thought her beautiful before, he thought her a thousand times more beautiful now that her eyes looked into his.

"Listen," said she. "I have been asleep for hundreds upon hundreds of years, for so it was fated to be until he should come who was to bring me back to life again. You are he, and now you shall live with me forever. In this castle is the wealth gathered by the king of the genii, and it is greater than all the riches of the world. It and the castle likewise shall be yours. I can transport everything into any part of the world you choose, and can by my arts make you prince or king or emperor. Come."

"Stop," said Gebhart. "I must first do as my master bade me."

He led the way into the other room, the lady following him, and so they both stood together by the couch where the wise man lay. When the lady saw his face she cried out in a loud voice: "It is the great master! What are you going to do?"

"I am going to sprinkle his face with this water," said Gebhart.

"Stop!" said she. "Listen to what I have to say. In your hand you hold the water of life and the dagger of death. The master is not dead, but sleeping; if you sprinkle that water upon him he will awaken, young, handsome and more powerful than the greatest magician that ever lived. I myself, this castle, and everything that is in it will be his, and, instead of your becoming a prince or a king or an emperor, he will be so in your place. That, I say, will happen if he wakens. Now the dagger of death is the only thing in the world that has power to kill him. You have it in your hand. You have but to give him one stroke with it while he sleeps, and he will never waken again, and then all will be yours—your very own."

Gebhart neither spoke nor moved, but stood looking down upon his master. Then he set down the goblet very softly on the floor, and, shutting his eyes that he might not see the blow, he raised the dagger to strike.

"That is all your promises amount to," said Nicholas Flamel the wise man. "After all, Babette, you need not bring the bread and cheese, for he shall be no pupil of mine."

Then Gebhart opened his eyes.

There sat the wise man in the midst of his books and bottles and diagrams and dust and chemicals and cobwebs, making strange figures upon the table with jackstraws and a piece of chalk.

And Babette, who had just opened the cupboard door for the loaf of bread and the cheese, shut it again with a bang, and went back to her spinning.

So Gebhart had to go back again to his Greek and Latin and algebra and geometry; for, after all, one cannot pour a gallon of beer into a quart pot, or the wisdom of a Nicholas Flamel into such a one as Gebhart.

As for the name of this story, why, if some promises are not bottles full of nothing but wind, there is little need to have a name for anything.

"SINCE we are in the way of talking of fools," said the Fisherman who drew the Genie out of the sea—"since we are in the way of talking of fools, I can tell you a story of the fool of all fools, and how, one after the other, he wasted as good gifts as a man's ears ever heard tell of."

"What was his name?" said the Lad who fiddled for the Devil in the bramble-bush.

"That," said the Fisherman, "I do not know."

"And what is this story about?" asked St. George.

"'Tis," said the Fisherman, "about a hole in the ground."

"And is that all?" said the Soldier who cheated the Devil.

"Nay," said the Fisherman, blowing a whiff from his pipe; "there were some things in the hole—a bowl of treasure, an earthen-ware jar, and a pair of candlesticks."

"And what do you call your story?" said St. George.

"Why," said the Fisherman, "for lack of a better name I will call it—

GOOD GIFTS AND A FOOL'S FOLLY

Give a fool heaven and earth, and all the stars,
and he will make ducks and drakes of them.

Once upon a time there was an old man, who, by thrifty living and long saving, had laid by a fortune great enough to buy ease and comfort and pleasure for a lifetime.

By-and-by he died, and the money came to his son, who was of a different sort from the father; for, what that one had gained by the labor of a whole year, the other spent in riotous living in one week.

So it came about in a little while that the young man found himself without so much as a single penny to bless himself withal. Then his fair-weather friends left him, and the creditors came and seized upon his house and his household

goods, and turned him out into the cold wide world to get along as best he might with the other fools who lived there.

Now the young spendthrift was a strong, stout fellow, and, seeing nothing better to do, he sold his fine clothes and bought him a porter's basket, and went and sat in the corner of the marketplace to hire himself out to carry this or that for folk who were better off in the world, and less foolish than he.

There he sat, all day long, from morning until evening, but nobody came to hire him. But at last, as dusk was settling, there came along an old man with beard as white as snow hanging down below his waist. He stopped in front of the foolish spendthrift, and stood looking at him for a while; then, at last, seeming to be satisfied, he beckoned with his finger to the young man. "Come," said he, "I have a task for you to do, and if you are wise, and keep a still tongue in your head, I will pay you as never a porter was paid before."

You may depend upon it the young man needed no second bidding to such a matter. Up he rose, and took his basket, and followed the old man, who led the way up one street and down another, until at last they came to a rickety, ramshackle house in a part of the town the young man had never been before. Here the old man stopped and knocked at the door, which was instantly opened, as though of itself, and then he entered with the young spendthrift at his heels. The two passed through a dark passage-way, and another door, and then, lo and behold! All was changed; for they had come suddenly into such a place as the young man would not have believed could be in such a house, had he not seen it with his own eyes. Thousands of waxen tapers lit the place as bright as day—a great oval room, floored with mosaic of a thousand bright colors and strange figures, and hung with tapestries of silks and satins and gold and silver. The ceiling was painted to represent the sky, through which flew beautiful birds and winged figures so life-like that no one could tell that they were only painted, and not real. At the farther side of the room were two richly cushioned couches, and thither the old man led the way with the young spendthrift following, wonder-struck, and there the two sat themselves down. Then the old man smote his hands together, and, in answer, ten young men and ten beautiful girls entered bearing a feast of rare fruits and wines which they spread before them, and the young man, who had been fasting since morning, fell to and ate as he had not eaten for many a day.

The old man, who himself ate but little, waited patiently for the other to end. "Now," said he, as soon as the young man could eat no more, "you have feasted and you have drunk; it is time for us to work."

Thereupon he rose from the couch and led the way, the young man following, through an arched doorway into a garden, in the center of which was an open space paved with white marble, and in the center of that again a carpet, ragged and worn, spread out upon the smooth stones. Without saying a word, the old man seated himself upon one end of this carpet, and motioned to the spendthrift to seat himself with his basket at the other end; then—

"Are you ready?" said the old man.

"Yes," said the young man, "I am."

"Then, by the horn of Jacob," said the old man, "I command thee, O Carpet! to bear us over hill and valley, over lake and river, to that spot whither I wish to go." Hardly had the words left his mouth when away flew the carpet, swifter than the swiftest wind, carrying the old man and the young spendthrift, until at last it brought them to a rocky desert without leaf or blade of grass to be seen far or near. Then it descended to where there was a circle of sand as smooth as a floor.

The old man rolled up the carpet, and then drew from a pouch that hung at his side a box, and from the box some sticks of sandal and spice woods, with which he built a little fire. Next he drew from the same pouch a brazen jar, from which he poured a gray powder upon the blaze. Instantly there leaped up a great flame of white light and a cloud of smoke, which rose high in the air, and there spread out until it hid everything from sight. Then the old man began to mutter spells, and in answer the earth shook and quaked, and a rumbling as of thunder filled the air. At last he gave a loud cry, and instantly the earth split open, and there the young spendthrift saw a trap-door of iron, in which was an iron ring to lift it by.

"Look!" said the old man. "Yonder is the task for which I have brought you; lift for me that trap-door of iron, for it is too heavy for me to raise, and I will pay you well."

And it was no small task, either, for, stout and strong as the young man was, it was all he could do to lift up the iron plate. But at last up it swung, and down below he saw a flight of stone steps leading into the earth.

The old man drew from his bosom a copper lamp, which he lit at the fire of the sandal and spice wood sticks, which had now nearly died away. Then, leading the way, with the young man following close at his heels, he descended the stairway that led down below. At the bottom the two entered a great vaulted room, carved out of the solid stone, upon the walls of which were painted strange pictures in bright colors of kings and queens, genii and dragons. Excepting for these painted figures, the vaulted room was perfectly bare, only that in the center of the floor there stood three stone tables. Upon the first table stood an iron candlestick with three branches; upon the second stood an earthen jar, empty of everything but dust; upon the third stood a brass bowl, a yard wide and a yard deep, and filled to the brim with shining, gleaming, dazzling jewels of all sorts.

"Now," said the old man to the spendthrift, "I will do to you as I promised: I will pay you as never man was paid before for such a task. Yonder upon those three stone tables are three great treasures: choose whichever one you will, and it is yours."

"I shall not be long in choosing," cried the young spendthrift. "I shall choose the brass bowl of jewels."

The old man laughed. "So be it," said he. "Fill your basket from the bowl with all you can carry, and that will be enough, provided you live wisely, to make you rich for as long as you live."

The young man needed no second bidding, but began filling his basket with both hands, until he had in it as much as he could carry.

Then the old man, taking the iron candlestick and the earthen jar, led the way up the stairway again. There the young man lowered the iron trap-door to its place, and so soon as he had done so the other stamped his heel upon the ground, and the earth closed of itself as smooth and level as it had been before.

The two sat themselves upon the carpet, the one upon the

one end, and the other upon the other. "By the horn of Jacob," said the old man, "I command thee, O Carpet! to fly over hill and valley, over lake and river, until thou hast brought us back whence we came."

Away flew the carpet, and in a little time they were back in the garden from which they had started upon their journey; and there they parted company. "Go thy way, young man," said the old graybeard, "and henceforth try to live more wisely than thou hast done heretofore. I know well who thou art, and how thou hast lived. Shun thy evil companions, live soberly, and thou hast enough to make thee rich for as long as thou livest."

"Have no fear," cried the young man, joyfully. "I have learned a bitter lesson, and henceforth I will live wisely and well."

So, filled with good resolves, the young man went the next day to his creditors and paid his debts; he bought back the house that his father had left him, and there began to lead a new life as he had promised.

But a gray goose does not become white, nor a foolish man a wise one.

At first he led a life sober enough; but by little and little he began to take up with his old-time friends again, and by-and-by the money went flying as merrily as ever, only this time he was twenty times richer than he had been before, and he spent his money twenty times as fast. Every day there was feasting and drinking going on in his house, and roaring and rioting and dancing and singing. The wealth of a king could not keep up such a life forever, so by the end of a year and a half the last of the treasure was gone, and the young spendthrift was just as poor as ever. Then once again his friends left him as they had done before, and all that he could do was to rap his head and curse his folly.

At last, one morning, he plucked up courage to go to the old man who had helped him once before, to see whether he would not help him again. Rap! tap! tap! he knocked at the door, and who should open it but the old man himself. "Well," said the graybeard, "what do you want?"

"I want some help," said the spendthrift; and then he told him all, and the old man listened and stroked his beard.

"By rights," said he, when the young man had ended, "I should leave you alone in your folly; for it is plain to see that nothing can cure you of it. Nevertheless, as you helped me once, and as I have more than I shall need, I will share what I have with you. Come in and shut the door."

He led the way, the spendthrift following, to a little room all of bare stone, and in which were only three things—the magic carpet, the iron candlestick, and the earthen jar. This last the old man gave to the foolish spendthrift. "My friend," said he, "when you chose the money and jewels that day in the cavern, you chose the less for the greater. Here is a treasure that an emperor might well envy you. Whatever you wish for you will find by dipping your hand into the jar. Now go your way, and let what has happened cure you of your folly."

"It shall," cried the young man; "never again will I be so foolish as I have been!" And thereupon he went his way with another pocketful of good resolves.

The first thing he did when he reached home was to try the virtue of his jar. "I should like," said he, "to have a handful of just such treasure as I brought from the cavern over yonder." He dipped his hand into the jar, and when he brought it out again it was brimful of shining, gleaming, sparkling jewels. You can guess how he felt when he saw them.

Well, this time a whole year went by, during which the young man lived as soberly as a judge. But at the end of the twelvemonth he was so sick of wisdom that he loathed it as one loathes bitter drink. Then by little and little he began to take up with his old ways again, and to call his old cronies around, until at the end of another twelvemonth things were a hundred times worse and wilder than ever; for now what he had he had without end.

One day, when he and a great party of roisterers were shouting and making merry, he brought out his earthen-ware pot to show them the wonders of it; and to prove its virtue he gave to each guest whatever he wanted. "What will you have?"—"A handful of gold."—"Put your hand in and get it!"—"What will you have?"—"A fistful of pearls."—"Put your fist in and get them!"—"What will you have?"—"A necklace of diamonds."—"Dip into the jar and get it." And so he went from one to another, and each and every one got what he asked for, and such a shouting and hubbub those walls had never heard before.

Then the young man, holding the jar in his hands, began to dance and to sing: "O wonderful jar! O beautiful jar! O beloved jar!" and so on, his friends clapping their hands, and laughing and cheering him. At last, in the height of his folly, he balanced the earthen jar on his head, and began dancing around and around with it to show his dexterity.

Smash! Crash! The precious jar lay in fifty pieces on the stone floor, and the young man stood staring at the result of his folly with bulging eyes, while his friends roared and laughed and shouted louder than ever over his mishap. And again his treasure and his gay life were gone.

But what had been hard for him to do before was easier now. At the end of a week he was back at the old man's house, rapping on the door. This time the old man asked him never a word, but frowned as black as thunder.

"I know," said he, "what has happened to you. If I were wise I should let you alone in your folly; but once more I will have pity on you and will help you, only this time it shall be the last." Once more he led the way to the stone room, where were the iron candlestick and the magic carpet, and with him he took a good stout cudgel. He stood the candlestick in the middle of the room, and taking three candles from his pouch, thrust one into each branch. Then he struck a light, and lit the first candle. Instantly there appeared a little old man, clad in a long white robe, who began dancing and spinning around and around like a top. He lit the second candle, and a second old man appeared, and round and round he went, spinning like his brother. He lit the third candle, and a third old man appeared. Around and around and around they spun and whirled, until the head spun and whirled to look at them. Then the old graybeard gripped the cudgel in his hand. "Are you ready?" he asked.

"We are ready, and waiting," answered the three. Thereupon, without another word, the graybeard fetched each of the dancers a blow upon the head with might and main—One! two! three! crack! crash! jingle!

Lo and behold! Instead of the three dancing men, there lay three great heaps of gold upon the floor, and the spendthrift stood staring like an owl. "There," said the old man, "take what you want, and then go your way, and trouble me no more."

"Well," said the spendthrift, "of all the wonders that ever I saw, this is the most wonderful! But how am I to carry my gold away with me, seeing I did not fetch my basket?"

"You shall have a basket," said the old man, "if only you will trouble me no more. Just wait here a moment until I bring it to you."

The spendthrift was left all alone in the room; not a soul was there but himself. He looked up, and he looked down, and scratched his head. "Why," he cried aloud, "should I be content to take a part when I can have the whole?"

To do was as easy as to say. He snatched up the iron candlestick, caught up the staff that the old man had left leaning against the wall, and seated himself upon the magic carpet. "By the horn of Jacob," he cried, "I command thee, O Carpet! to carry me over hill and valley, over lake and river, to a place where the old man can never find me."

Hardly had the words left his mouth than away flew the carpet through the air, carrying him along with it; away and away, higher than the clouds and swifter than the wind. Then at last it descended to the earth again, and when the young spendthrift looked about him, he found himself in just such a desert place as he and the old man had come to when they had found the treasure. But he gave no thought to that, and hardly looked around him to see where he was. All that he thought of was to try his hand at the three dancers that belonged to the candlestick. He struck a light, and lit the three candles, and instantly the three little old men appeared for him just as they had for the old graybeard. And around and around they spun and whirled, until the sand and dust spun and whirled along with them. Then the young man grasped his cudgel tightly.

Now, he had not noticed that when the old man struck the three dancers he had held the cudgel in his *left* hand, for he was not wise enough to know that great differences come from little matters. He gripped the cudgel in his right hand, and struck the dancers with might and main, just as the old man had done. Crack! Crack! Crack! One; two; three.

Did they change into piles of gold? Not a bit of it! Each of the dancers drew from under his robe a cudgel as stout and stouter than the one the young man himself held, and, without a word, fell upon him and began to beat and drub him until the dust flew. In vain he hopped and howled and begged for mercy, in vain he tried to defend himself; the three never stopped until he fell to the ground, and laid there panting and sighing and groaning; and then they left and flew back with the iron candlestick and the magic carpet to the old man again. At last, after a great while, the young spendthrift sat up, rubbing the sore places; but when he looked around not a sign was to be seen of anything but the stony desert, without a house or a man in sight.

Perhaps, after a long time, he found his way home again, and perhaps the drubbing he had had taught him wisdom; the first is a likely enough thing to happen, but as for the second, it would need three strong men to tell it to me a great many times before I would believe it.

You may smile at this story if you like, but, all the same, as certainly as there is meat in an egg-shell, so is there truth in this nonsense. For, "Give a fool heaven and earth," say I, "and all the stars, and he will make ducks and drakes of them."

FORTUNATUS lifted his canican to his lips and took a long, hearty draught of ale. "Methinks," said he, "that all your stories have a twang of the same sort about them. You all of you, except my friend the Soldier here, play the same tune upon a different fiddle. Nobody comes to any good."

St. George drew a long whiff of his pipe, and then puffed out a cloud of smoke as big as his head. "Perhaps," said he to Fortunatus, "you know of a story which turns out differently. If you do, let us have it, for it is your turn now."

"Very well," said Fortunatus, "I will tell you a story that turns out as it should, where the lad marries a beautiful princess and becomes a king into the bargain."

"And what is your story about?" said the Lad who fiddled for the Devil in the bramble-bush.

"It is," said Fortunatus, "about—

6

THE GOOD OF A FEW WORDS

There was one Beppo the Wise and another Beppo the Foolish.

The wise one was the father of the foolish one.

Beppo the Wise was called Beppo the Wise because he had laid up a great treasure after a long life of hard work.

Beppo the Foolish was called Beppo the Foolish because he spent in five years after his father was gone from this world of sorrow all that the old man had laid together in his long life of toil.

But during that time Beppo lived as a prince, and the like was never seen in that town before or since—feasting and drinking and junketing and merrymaking. He had friends by the dozen and by the scores, and the fame of his doings went throughout all the land.

While his money lasted he was called Beppo the Generous.

It was only after it was all gone that they called him Beppo the Foolish.

So by-and-by the money was spent, and there was an end of it.

Yes; there was an end of it; and where were all of Beppo's fair-weather friends? Gone like the wild-geese in frosty weather.

"Don't you remember how I gave you a bagful of gold?" said Beppo the Foolish. "Won't you remember me now in my time of need?"

But the fair-weather friend only laughed in his face.

"Don't you remember how I gave you a fine gold chain with a diamond pendant?" said Beppo to another. "And won't you lend me a little money to help me over today?"

But the summer-goose friend only grinned.

"But what shall I do to keep body and soul together?" said Beppo to a third.

The man was a wit. "Go to a shoemaker," said he, "and let him stitch the soul fast"; and that was all the good Beppo had of him.

Then poor Beppo saw that there was no place for him in that town, and so off he went to seek his fortune else-whither, for he saw that there was nothing to be gained in that place.

So he journeyed on for a week and a day, and then towards evening he came to the king's town.

There it stood on the hill beside the river—the grandest city in the kingdom. There were orchards and plantations of trees along the banks of the stream, and gardens and summer-houses and pavilions. There were white houses and red roofs and blue skies. Up above on the hill were olive orchards and fields, and then blue sky again.

Beppo went into the town, gazing about him with admiration. Houses, palaces, gardens. He had never seen the like. Stores and shops full of cloths of velvet and silk and satin; goldsmiths, silversmiths, jewelers—as though all the riches of the world had been emptied into the city. Crowds of people— lords, noblemen, courtiers, rich merchants, and tradesmen.

Beppo stared about at the fine sights and everybody stared at Beppo, for his shoes were dusty, his clothes were travel-stained, and a razor had not touched his face for a week.

The king of that country was walking in the garden under the shade of the trees, and the sunlight slanted down upon him, and sparkled upon the jewels around his neck and on his fingers. Two dogs walked alongside of him, and a whole crowd of lords and nobles and courtiers came behind him; first of all the prime-minister with his long staff.

But for all this fine show this king was not really the king.

When the old king died he left a daughter, and she should have been queen if she had had her own rights. But this king, who was her uncle, had stepped in before her, and so the poor princess was pushed aside and was nobody at all but a princess, the king's niece.

She stood on the terrace with her old nurse, while the king walked in the garden below.

It had been seven years now since the old king had died, and in that time she had grown up into a beautiful young woman, as wise as she was beautiful, and as good as she was wise. Few people ever saw her, but everybody talked about her in whispers and praised her beauty and goodness, saying that, if the right were done, she would have her own and be queen.

Sometimes the king heard of this (for a king hears everything), and he grew to hate the princess as a man hates bitter drink.

The princess looked down from the terrace, and there she saw Beppo walking along the street, and his shoes were dusty and his clothes were travel-stained, and a razor had not touched his face for a week.

"Look at yonder poor man," she said to her nurse; "yet if I were his wife he would be greater really than my uncle, the king."

The king, walking below in the garden, heard what she said.

"Say you so!" he called out. "Then we shall try if what you say is true"; and he turned away, shaking with anger.

"Alas!" said the princess, "now, indeed, have I ruined myself for good and all."

Beppo was walking along the street looking about him hither and thither, and thinking how fine it all was. He had no more thought that the king and the princess were talking about him than the man on the moon.

Suddenly someone clapped him upon the shoulder.

Beppo turned around.

There stood a great tall man dressed in all black.

"You must come with me," said he.

"What do you want with me?" said Beppo.

"That you shall see for yourself," said the man.

"Very well," said Beppo; "I'd as lief go along with you as anywhere else."

So he turned and followed the man whither he led.

They went along first one street and then another, and by-and-by they came to the river, and there was a long wall with a gate in it. The tall man in black knocked upon the gate, and someone opened it from within. The man in black entered, and Beppo followed at his heels, wondering where he was going.

He was in a garden. There were fruit trees and flowering shrubs and long marble walks, and away in the distance a great grand palace of white marble that shone red as fire in the light of the setting sun, but there was not a soul to be seen anywhere.

The tall man in black led the way up the long marble walk, past the fountains and fruit trees and beds of roses, until he had come to the palace.

Beppo wondered whether he were dreaming.

The tall man in black led the way into the palace, but still there was not a soul to be seen.

Beppo gazed about him in wonder. There were floors of colored marble, and ceilings of blue and gold, and columns of carved marble, and hangings of silk and velvet and silver.

Suddenly the tall man opened a little door that led into a dark passage, and Beppo followed him. They went along the passage, and then the man opened another door.

Then Beppo found himself in a great vaulted room. There at one end of the room were three souls. A man sat on the throne, and he was the king, for he had a crown on his head and a long robe over his shoulders. Beside him stood a priest, and in front of him stood a beautiful young woman as white as wax and as still as death.

Beppo wondered whether he were awake.

"Come hither," said the king, in a harsh voice, and Beppo

came forward and kneeled before him. "Take this young woman by the hand," said the king.

Beppo did as he was bidden.

Her hand was as cold as ice.

Then, before Beppo knew what was happening, he found that he was being married.

It was the princess.

"Now," said the king to her when the priest had ended, and he frowned until his brows were as black as thunder—"now you are married; tell me, is your husband greater than I?"

But the princess said never a word, only the tears ran one after another down her white face. The king sat staring at her and frowning.

Suddenly some one tapped Beppo upon the shoulder. It was the tall man in black.

Beppo knew that he was to follow him again. This time the princess was to go along. The tall man in black led the way, and Beppo and the princess followed along the secret passage and up and down the stairs until at last they came out into the garden again.

And now the evening was beginning to fall.

The man led the way down the garden to the river, and still Beppo and the princess followed him.

By-and-by they came to the river-side and to a flight of steps, and there was a little frail boat without sail or oars.

The tall man in black beckoned towards the boat, and Beppo knew that he and the princess were to enter it.

As soon as Beppo had helped the princess into the boat the tall man thrust it out into the stream with his foot, and the boat drifted away from the shore and out into the river, and then around and around. Then it floated off down the stream.

It floated on and on, and the sun set and the moon rose.

Beppo looked at the princess, and he thought he had never seen any one so beautiful in all his life. It was all like a dream, and he hoped he might never awaken. But the princess sat there weeping and weeping, and said nothing.

The night fell darker and darker, but still Beppo sat looking at the princess. Her face was as white as silver in the moonlight. The smell of the flower-gardens came across the river. The boat floated on and on until by-and-by it drifted to the shore again and among the river reeds, and there it stopped, and Beppo carried the princess ashore.

"Listen," said the princess. "Do you know who I am?"

"No," said Beppo, "I do not."

"I am the princess," said she, "the king's niece; and by rights I should be queen of this land."

Beppo could not believe his ears.

"It is true that I am married to you," said she, "but never shall you be my husband until you are king."

"King!" said Beppo; "how can I be king?"

"You shall be king," said the princess.

"But the king is everything," said Beppo, "and I am nothing at all."

"Great things come from small beginnings," said the princess; "a big tree from a little seed."

Some little distance away from the river was the twinkle of a light, and thither Beppo led the princess. When the two came to it, they found it was a little hut, for there were fish-nets hanging outside in the moonlight.

Beppo knocked.

An old woman opened the door. She stared and stared, as well she might, to see the fine lady in silks and satins with a gold ring upon her finger, and nobody with her but one who looked like a poor beggar-man.

"Who are you and what do you want?" said the old woman.

"Who we are," said the princess, "does not matter, except that we are honest folk in trouble. What we want is shelter for the night and food to eat, and that we will pay for."

"Shelter I can give you," said the old woman, "but little

else but a crust of bread and a cup of water. One time there was enough and plenty in the house; but now, since my husband has gone and I am left all alone, it is little I have to eat and drink. But such as I have to give you are welcome to."

Then Beppo and the princess went into the house.

The next morning the princess called Beppo to her. "Here," said she, "is a ring and a letter. Go you into the town and inquire for Sebastian the Goldsmith. He will know what to do."

Beppo took the ring and the letter and started off to town, and it was not hard for him to find the man he sought, for every one knew of Sebastian the Goldsmith. He was an old man, with a great white beard and a forehead like the dome of a temple. He looked at Beppo from head to foot with eyes as bright as those of a snake; then he took the ring and the letter. As soon as he saw the ring he raised it to his lips and kissed it; then he kissed the letter also; then he opened it and read it.

He turned to Beppo and bowed very low. "My lord," said he, "I will do as I am commanded. Will you be pleased to follow me?"

He led the way into an inner room. There were soft rugs upon the floor, and around the walls were tapestries. There were couches and silken cushions. Beppo wondered what it all meant.

Sebastian the Goldsmith clapped his hands together. A door opened, and there came three slaves into the room. The Goldsmith spoke to them in a strange language, and the chief of the three slaves bowed in reply. Then he and the others led Beppo into another room where there was a marble bath of tepid water. They bathed him and rubbed him with soft linen towels; then they shaved the beard from his cheeks and chin and trimmed his hair; then they clothed him in fine linen and a plain suit of gray and Beppo looked like a new man.

Then when all this was done the chief conducted Beppo back to Sebastian the Goldsmith. There was a fine feast spread, with fruit and wine. Beppo sat down to it, and Sebastian the Goldsmith stood and served him with a napkin over his arm.

Then Beppo was to return to the princess again.

A milk-white horse was waiting for him at the Goldsmith's door, a servant holding the bridle, and Beppo mounted and rode away.

When he returned to the fisherman's hut the princess was waiting for him. She had prepared a tray spread with a napkin, a cup of milk, and some sweet cakes.

"Listen," said she; "today the king hunts in the forest over yonder. Go you thither with this. The king will be hot and thirsty, and weary with the chase. Offer him this refreshment. He will eat and drink, and in gratitude he will offer you something in return. Take nothing of him, but ask him this: that he allow you once every three days to come to the palace, and that he whisper these words in your ear so that no one else may hear them—'A word, a word, only a few words; spoken ill, they are ill; spoken well, they are more precious than gold and jewels.'"

"Why should I do that?" said Beppo.

"You will see," said the princess.

Beppo did not understand it at all, but the princess is a princess and must be obeyed, and so he rode away on his horse at her bidding.

It was as the princess had said: the king was hunting in the forest, and when Beppo came there he could hear the shouts of the men and the winding of horns and the baying of dogs. He waited there for maybe an hour or more, and sometimes the sounds were nearer and sometimes the sounds were farther away. Presently they came nearer and nearer, and then all of a sudden the king came riding out of the forest, the hounds hunting hither and thither, and the lords and nobles and courtiers following him.

The king's face was flushed and heated with the chase, and his forehead was bedewed with sweat. Beppo came forward and offered the tray. The king wiped his face with the napkin, and then drank the milk and ate three of the cakes.

"Who was it ordered you to bring this to me?" said he to Beppo.

"No one," said Beppo; "I brought it myself."

The king looked at Beppo and was grateful to him.

"Thou hast given me pleasure and comfort," said he; "ask what thou wilt in return and if it is in reason thou shalt have it."

"I will have only this," said Beppo: "that your majesty will allow me once every three days to come to the palace, and that then you will take me aside and will whisper these words into my ear so that no one else may hear them—'A word, a word, only a few words; spoken ill, they are ill; spoken well, they are more precious than gold and jewels.'"

The king burst out laughing. "Why," said he, "what is this foolish thing you ask of me? If you had asked for a hundred pieces of gold you should have had them. Think better, friend, and ask something of more worth than this foolish thing."

"Please your majesty," said Beppo, "I ask nothing else."

The king laughed again. "Then you shall have what you ask," said he, and he rode away.

The next morning the princess said to Beppo: "This day you shall go and claim the king's promise of him. Take this ring and this letter again to Sebastian the Goldsmith. He will fit you with clothes in which to appear before the king. Then go to the king's palace that he may whisper those words he has to say into your ear."

Once more Beppo went to Sebastian the Goldsmith, and the Goldsmith kissed the princess's ring and letter, and then read what she had written.

Again the slaves took Beppo to the bath, only this time they clad him in a fine suit of velvet and hung a gold chain about his neck. After that Sebastian the Goldsmith again served a feast to Beppo, and waited upon him while he ate and drank.

In front of the house a noble horse, as black as jet, was waiting to carry Beppo to the palace, and two servants dressed in velvet livery were waiting to attend him.

So Beppo rode away, and many people stopped to look at him.

He came to the palace, and the king was giving audience. Beppo went into the great audience-chamber. It was full of people—lords and nobles and rich merchants and lawyers.

Beppo did not know how to come to the king, so he stood there and waited and waited. The people looked at him and whispered to one another: "Who is that young man?" "Whence comes he?" Then one said: "Is not he the young man who served the king with cakes and milk in the forest yesterday?"

Beppo stood there gazing at the king. By-and-by the king suddenly looked up and caught sight of him. He gazed at Beppo for a moment or two and then he knew him. Then he smiled and beckoned to him.

"Aye, my foolish benefactor," said he, aloud, "is it thou, and art thou come so soon to redeem thy promise? Very well; come hither, I have something to say to thee."

Beppo came forward, and everybody stared. He came close to the king, and the king laid his hand upon his shoulder. Then he leaned over to Beppo and whispered in his ear: "A word, a word, only a few words; if they be spoken ill, they are ill; if they be spoken well, they are more precious than gold and jewels." Then he laughed. "Is that what you would have me say?" said he.

"Yes, majesty," said Beppo, and he bowed low and withdrew.

But, lo and behold, what a change!

Suddenly he was transformed in the eyes of the whole world. The crowd drew back to allow him to pass, and everybody bowed low as he went along.

"Did you not see the king whisper to him," said one. "What could it be that the king said?" said another. "This must be a new favorite," said a third.

He had come into the palace Beppo the Foolish; he went

forth Beppo the Great Man, and all because of a few words the king had whispered in his ear.

Three days passed, and then Beppo went again to the Goldsmith's with the ring and a letter from the princess. This time Sebastian the Goldsmith fitted him with a suit of splendid plum-colored silk and gave him a dappled horse, and again Beppo and his two attendants rode away to the palace. And this time every one knew him, and as he went up the steps into the palace all present bowed to him. The king saw him as soon as he appeared, and when he caught sight of him he burst out laughing.

"Aye," said he, "I was looking for thee today, and wondering how soon thou wouldst come. Come hither till I whisper something in thine ear."

Then all the lords and nobles and courtiers and ministers drew back, and Beppo went up to the king.

The king laughed and laughed. He laid his arm over Beppo's shoulder, and again he whispered in his ear: "A word, a word, only a few words; if they be spoken ill, they are ill; if they be spoken well, they are more precious than gold and jewels."

Then he released Beppo, and Beppo withdrew.

So it continued for three months. Every three days Beppo went to the palace, and the king whispered the words in his ear. Beppo said nothing to any one, and always went away as soon as the king had whispered to him.

Then at last the princess said to him: "Now the time is ripe for doing. Listen! Today when you go to the palace fix your eyes, when the king speaks to you, upon the prime-minister, and shake your head. The prime-minister will ask you what the king said. Say nothing to him but this: 'Alas, my poor friend!'"

It was all just as the princess had said.

The king was walking in the garden, with his courtiers and ministers about him. Beppo came to him, and the king, as he always did, laid his hand upon Beppo's shoulder and whispered in his ear: "A word, a word, only a few words; if they be spoken ill, they are ill; if they be spoken well, they are more precious than gold and jewels."

While the king was saying these words to Beppo, Beppo was looking fixedly at the prime-minister. While he did so he shook his head three times. Then he bowed low and walked away.

He had not gone twenty paces before some one tapped him upon the arm; it was the prime-minister. Beppo gazed fixedly at him. "Alas, my poor friend!" said he.

The prime-minister turned pale. "It was, then, as I thought," said he. "The king spoke about me. Will you not tell me what he said?"

Beppo shook his head. "Alas, my poor friend!" said he, and then he walked on.

The prime-minister still followed him.

"My lord," said he, "I have been aware that his majesty has not been the same to me for more than a week past. If it was about the princess, pray tell his majesty that I meant nothing ill when I spoke of her to him."

Beppo shook his head. "Alas, my poor friend!" he said.

The prime-minister's lips trembled. "My lord," said he, "I have always had the kindest regard for you, and if there is anything in my power that I can do for you I hope you will command me. I know how much you are in his majesty's confidence. Will you not speak a few words to set the matter straight?"

Beppo again shook his head. "Alas, my poor friend!" said he, and then he got upon his horse and rode away.

Three days passed.

"This morning," said the princess, "when you go to the king, look at the prime-minister when the king speaks to you, and smile. The prime-minister will again speak to you, and this time say, 'It is well, and I wish you joy.' Take what he gives you, for it will be of use."

Again all happened just as the princess said.

Beppo came to the palace, and again the king whispered in

his ear. As he did so Beppo looked at the prime-minister and smiled, and then he withdrew.

The prime-minister followed him. He trembled. "It is well," said Beppo, "and I wish you joy."

The prime-minister grasped his hand and wrung it. "My lord," said he, "how can I express my gratitude! The palace of my son that stands by the river—I would that you would use it for your own, if I may be so bold as to offer it to you."

"I will," said Beppo, "use it as my own."

The prime-minister wrung his hand again, and then Beppo rode away.

The next time that Beppo spoke to the king, at the princess's bidding, he looked at the lord-treasurer, and said, as he had said to the prime-minister, "Alas, my poor friend!"

When he rode away he left the lord-treasurer as white as ashes to the very lips.

Three days passed, and then, while the king talked to Beppo, Beppo looked at the lord-treasurer and smiled.

The lord-treasurer followed him to the door of the palace.

"It is well, and I wish you joy," said Beppo.

The treasurer offered him a fortune.

The next time it was the same with the captain of the guards. First Beppo pitied him, and then he wished him joy.

"My lord," said the captain of the guards, "my services are yours at any time."

Then the same thing happened to the governor of the city, then to this lord, and then to that lord.

Beppo grew rich and powerful beyond measure.

Then one day the princess said: "Now we will go into the town, and to the palace of the prime-minister's son, which the prime-minister gave you, for the time is ripe for the end."

In a few days all the court knew that Beppo was living like a prince in the prime-minister's palace. The king began to wonder what it all meant, and how all such good-fortune had come to Beppo. He had grown very tired of always speaking to Beppo the same words.

But Beppo was now great among the great; all the world paid court to him, and bowed down to him, almost as they did before the king.

"Now," said the princess, "the time has come to strike. Bid all the councilors, and all the lords, and all the nobles to meet here three days hence, for it is now or never that you shall win all and become king."

Beppo did as she bade. He asked all of the great people of the kingdom to come to him, and they came. When they were all gathered together at Beppo's house, they found two thrones set as though for a king and a queen, but there was no sign of Beppo, and everybody wondered what it all meant.

Suddenly the door opened and Beppo came into the room, leading by the hand a lady covered with a veil from head to foot.

Everybody stopped speaking and stood staring while Beppo led the veiled lady up to one of the thrones. He seated himself upon the other.

The lady stood up and dropped her veil, and then every one knew her.

It was the princess.

"Do you not know me?" said she; "I am the queen, and this is my husband. He is your king."

All stood silent for a moment, and then a great shout went up. "Long live the queen! Long live the king!"

The princess turned to the captain of the guards. "You have offered your services to my husband," said she; "his commands and my commands are that you march to the palace and cast out him who hath no right there."

"It shall be done," said the captain of the guards.

All the troops were up in arms, and the town was full of tumult and confusion. About midnight they brought the false

king before King Beppo and the queen. The false king stood there trembling like a leaf. The queen stood gazing at him steadily. "Behold, this is the husband that thou gavest me," said she. "It is as I said; he is greater than thou. For, lo, he is king! What art thou?"

The false king was banished out of the country, and the poor fisherman's wife, who had entertained the princess for all this time, came to live at the palace, where all was joy and happiness.

"FRIEND," said St. George, "I like your story. Nevertheless, 'tis like a strolling peddler, in that it carries a great pack of ills to begin with, to get rid of 'em all before it gets to the end of its journey. However, 'tis as you say—it ends with everybody merry and feasting, and so I like it. But now methinks our little friend yonder is big with a story of his own"; and he pointed, as he spoke, with the stem of his pipe to a little man whom I knew was the brave Tailor who had killed seven flies at a blow, for he still had around his waist the bell with the legend that he himself had worked upon it.

"Aye," piped the Tailor in a keen, high voice, "'tis true I have a story inside of me. 'Tis about another tailor who had a great, big, ugly demon to wait upon him and to sew his clothes for him."

"And the name of that story, my friend," said the Soldier who had cheated the Devil, "is what?"

"It hath no name," piped the little Tailor, "but I will give it one, and it shall be—

WOMAN'S WIT

When man's strength fails,
woman's wit prevails.

In the days when the great and wise King Solomon lived and ruled, evil spirits and demons were as plentiful in the world as wasps in summer.

So King Solomon, who was so wise and knew so many potent spells that he had power over evil such as no man has had before or since, set himself to work to put those enemies of mankind out of the way. Some he conjured into bottles, and sank into the depths of the sea; some he buried in the earth; some he destroyed altogether, as one burns hair in a candle-flame.

Now, one pleasant day when King Solomon was walking in his garden with his hands behind his back, and his thoughts busy as bees with this or that, he came face to face with a Demon, who was a prince of his kind. "Ho, little man," cried the evil spirit, in a loud voice, "art not thou the wise King Solomon who conjures my brethren into brass chests and glass bottles? Come, try a fall at wrestling with me, and whoever conquers shall be master over the other for all time. What do you say to such an offer as that?"

"I say aye!" said King Solomon, and, without another word, he stripped off his royal robes and stood bare breasted, man to man with the other.

The world never saw the like of that wrestling match betwixt the king and the Demon, for they struggled and strove together from the seventh hour in the morning to the sunset in the evening, and during that time the sky was clouded over as black as night, and the lightning forked and shot, and the thunder roared and bellowed, and the earth shook and quaked.

But at last the king gave the enemy an undertwist, and flung him down on the earth so hard that the apples fell from the trees; and then, panting and straining, he held the evil one down, knee on neck. Thereupon the sky presently cleared again, and all was as pleasant as a spring day.

King Solomon bound the Demon with spells, and made him serve him for seven years. First, he had him build a splendid palace, the like of which was not to be seen within the bounds of the seven rivers; then he made him set around the palace a garden, such as I for one wish I may see some time or other. Then, when the Demon had done all that the king wished, the king conjured him into a bottle, corked it tightly, and set the royal seal on the stopper. Then he took the bottle a thousand miles away into the wilderness, and, when no man was looking, buried it in the ground, and this is the way the story begins.

Well, the years came and the years went, and the world grew older and older, and kept changing (as all things do but two), so that by-and-by the wilderness where King Solomon had hid the bottle became a great town, with people coming and going, and all as busy as bees about their own business and other folks' affairs.

Among these towns-people was a little Tailor, who made clothes for many a worse man to wear, and who lived all alone in a little house with no one to darn his stockings for him, and no one to meddle with his coming and going, for he was a bachelor.

The little Tailor was a thrifty soul, and by hook and crook had laid by enough money to fill a small pot, and then he had to bethink himself of some safe place to hide it. So one night he took a spade and a lamp and went out in the garden to bury his money. He drove his spade into the ground—and click! He struck something hard that rang under his foot with a sound as of iron. "Hello!" said he, "what have we here?" and if he had known as much as you and I do, he would have filled in the earth, and tramped it down, and have left that plate of broth for somebody else to burn his mouth with.

As it was, he scraped away the soil, and then he found a box of adamant, with a ring in the lid to lift it by. The Tailor clutched the ring and bent his back, and up came the box with the damp earth sticking to it. He cleaned the mold away, and there he saw, written in red letters, these words:

"Open not."

You may be sure that after he had read these words he was not long in breaking open the lid of the box with his spade.

Inside the first box he found a second, and upon it the same words:

"Open not."

Within the second box was another, and within that still another, until there were seven in all, and on each was written the same words:

"Open not."

Inside the seventh box was a roll of linen, and inside that a bottle filled with nothing but blue smoke; and I wish that bottle had burned the Tailor's fingers when he touched it.

"And is this all?" said the little Tailor, turning the bottle upside down and shaking it, and peeping at it by the light of the lamp. "Well, since I have gone so far I might as well open it, as I have already opened the seven boxes." Thereupon he broke the seal that stoppered it.

Pop! Out flew the cork, and—Puff! Out came the smoke; not all at once, but in a long thread that rose up as high as the stars, and then spread until it hid their light.

The Tailor stared and goggled and gaped to see so much smoke come out of such a little bottle, and, as he goggled and stared, the smoke began to gather together again, thicker and thicker, and darker and darker, until it was as black as ink. Then out from it there stepped one with eyes that shone like sparks of fire, and who had a countenance so terrible that the Tailor's skin quivered and shriveled, and his tongue clove to the roof of his mouth at the sight of it.

"Who art thou?" said the terrible being, in a voice that made the very marrow of the poor Tailor's bones turn soft from terror.

"If you please, sir," said he, "I am only a little tailor."

The evil being lifted up both hands and eyes. "How

wonderful," he cried, "that one little tailor can undo in a moment that which took the wise Solomon a whole day to accomplish, and in the doing of which he well-nigh broke the sinews of his heart!" Then, turning to the Tailor, who stood trembling like a rabbit, "Hark thee!" said he. "For two thousand years I lay there in that bottle, and no one came nigh to aid me. Thou hast liberated me, and thou shalt not go unrewarded. Every morning at the seventh hour I will come to thee, and I will perform for thee whatever task thou mayest command me. But there is one condition attached to the agreement, and woe be to thee if that condition is broken. If any morning I should come to thee, and thou hast no task for me to do, I shall wring thy neck as thou mightest wring the neck of a sparrow." Thereupon he was gone in an instant, leaving the little Tailor half dead with terror.

Now it happened that the prime-minister of that country had left an order with the Tailor for a suit of clothes, so the next morning, when the Demon came, the little man set him to work on the bench, with his legs tucked up like a journeyman tailor. "I want," said he, "such and such a suit of clothes."

"You shall have them," said the Demon; and thereupon he began snipping in the air, and cutting most wonderful patterns of silks and satins out of nothing at all, and the little Tailor sat and gaped and stared. Then the Demon began to drive the needle like a spark of fire—the like was never seen in all the seven kingdoms, for the clothes seemed to make themselves.

At last, at the end of a little while, the Demon stood up and brushed his hands.

"They are done," said he, and thereupon he instantly vanished. But the Tailor cared little for that, for upon the bench there lay such a suit of clothes of silk and satin stuff, sewed with threads of gold and silver and set with jewels, as the eyes of man never saw before; and the Tailor packed them up and marched off with them himself to the prime-minister.

The prime-minister wore the clothes to court that very day, and before evening they were the talk of the town. All the world ran to the Tailor and ordered clothes of him, and his fortune was made. Every day the Demon created new suits of clothes out of nothing at all, so that the Tailor grew rich, and held his head up in the world.

As time went along he laid heavier and heavier tasks upon the Demon's back, and demanded of him more and more; but all the while the Demon kept his own counsel, and said never a word.

One morning, as the Tailor sat in his shop window taking the world easy—for he had little or nothing to do now—he heard a great hubbub in the street below, and when he looked down he saw that it was the king's daughter passing by. It was

the first time that the Tailor had seen her, and when he saw her his heart stood still within him, and then began fluttering like a little bird, for one so beautiful was not to be met with in the four corners of the world. Then she was gone.

All that day the little Tailor could do nothing but sit and think of the princess, and the next morning when the Demon came he was thinking of her still.

"What hast thou for me to do today?" said the Demon, as he always said of a morning.

The little Tailor was waiting for the question.

"I would like you," said he, "to send to the king's palace, and to ask him to let me have his daughter for my wife."

"Thou shalt have thy desire," said the Demon. Thereupon he smote his hands together like a clap of thunder, and instantly the walls of the room clove asunder, and there came out four-and-twenty handsome youths, clad in cloth of gold and silver. After these four-and-twenty there came another one who was the chief of them all, and before whom, splendid as they were, the four-and-twenty paled like stars in daylight. "Go to the king's palace," said the Demon to that one, "and deliver this message: The Tailor of Tailors, the Master of Masters, and One Greater than a King asks for his daughter to wife."

"To hear is to obey," said the chief, and bowed his forehead to the earth.

Never was there such a hubbub in the town as when those five-and-twenty, in their clothes of silver and gold, rode through the streets to the king's palace. As they came near, the gates of the palace flew open before them, and the king himself came out to meet them. The leader of the four-and-twenty leaped from his horse, and, kissing the ground before the king, delivered his message: "The Tailor of Tailors, the Master of Masters, and One Greater than a King asks for thy daughter to wife."

When the king heard what the messenger said, he thought and pondered a long time. At last he said, "If he who sent you is the Master of Masters, and greater than a king, let him send me an asking gift such as no king could send."

"It shall be as you desire," said the messenger, and thereupon the five-and-twenty rode away as they had come, followed by crowds of people.

The next morning when the Demon came the tailor was ready and waiting for him. "What hast thou for me to do today?" said the Evil One.

"I want," said the tailor, "a gift to send to the king such as no other king could send him."

"Thou shalt have thy desire," said the Demon. Thereupon he smote his hands together, and summoned, not five-and-twenty young men, but fifty youths, all clad in clothes more splendid than the others.

All of the fifty sat upon coal-black horses, with saddles of silver and housings of silk and velvet embroidered with gold. In the midst of all the five-and-seventy there rode a youth in cloth of silver embroidered in pearls. In his hand he bore something wrapped in a white napkin, and that was the present for the king such as no other king could give. So said the Demon: "Take it to the royal palace, and tell his majesty that it is from the Tailor of Tailors, the Master of Masters, and One Greater than a King."

"To hear is to obey," said the young man, and then they all rode away.

When they came to the palace the gates flew open before them, and the king came out to meet them. The young man who bore the present dismounted and prostrated himself in the dust, and, when the king bade him arise, he unwrapped the napkin, and gave to the king a goblet made of one single ruby, and filled to the brim with pieces of gold. Moreover, the cup was of such a kind that whenever it was emptied of its money it instantly became full again. "The Tailor of Tailors, and Master of Masters, and One Greater than a King sends your majesty this goblet, and bids me, his ambassador, to ask for your daughter," said the young man.

When the king saw what had been sent him he was filled with amazement. "Surely," said he to himself, "there can be no end to the power of one who can give such a gift as this." Then to the messenger, "Tell your master that he shall have my daughter for his wife if he will build over yonder a palace such as no man ever saw or no king ever lived in before."

"It shall be done," said the young man, and then they all went away, as the others had done the day before.

The next morning when the Demon appeared the Tailor was ready for him. "Build me," said he, "such and such a palace in such and such a place."

And the Demon said, "It shall be done." He smote his hands together, and instantly there came a cloud of mist that covered and hid the spot where the palace was to be built. Out from the cloud there came such a banging and hammering and clapping and clattering as the people of that town never heard before. Then when evening had come the cloud arose, and there, where the king had pointed out, stood a splendid palace as white as snow, with roofs and domes of gold and silver. As the king stood looking and wondering at this sight, there came five hundred young men riding, and one in the midst of all who wore a golden crown on his head, and upon his body a long robe stiff with diamonds and pearls. "We come," said he, "from the Tailor of Tailors, and Master of Masters, and One Greater than a King, to ask you to let him have your daughter for his wife."

"Tell him to come!" cried the king, in admiration, "for the princess is his."

The next morning when the Demon came he found the Tailor dancing and shouting for joy. "The princess is mine!" he cried, "so make me ready for her."

"It shall be done," said the Demon, and thereupon he began to make the Tailor ready for his wedding. He brought him to a marble bath of water, in which he washed away all that was coarse and ugly, and from which the little man came forth as beautiful as the sun. Then the Demon clad him in the finest linen, and covered him with clothes such as even the emperor of India never wore. Then he smote his hands together, and the wall of the tailor-shop opened as it had done twice before, and there came forth forty slaves clad in crimson, and bearing bowls full of money in their hands. After them came two leading a horse as white as snow, with a saddle of gold studded with diamonds and rubies and emeralds and sapphires. After came a bodyguard of twenty warriors clad in gold armor. Then the Tailor mounted his horse and rode away to the king's palace, and as he rode the slaves scattered the money amongst the crowd, who scrambled for it and cheered the Tailor to the skies.

That night the princess and the Tailor were married, and all the town was lit with bonfires and fireworks. The two rode away in the midst of a great crowd of nobles and courtiers to the palace that the Demon had built for the Tailor; and, as the princess gazed upon him, she thought that she had never beheld so noble and handsome a man as her husband. So she and the Tailor were the happiest couple in the world.

But the next morning the Demon appeared as he had appeared ever since the Tailor had let him out of the bottle, only now he grinned till his teeth shone. "What hast thou for me to do?" said he, and at the words the Tailor's heart began to quake, for he remembered what was to happen to him when he could find the Demon no more work to do—that his neck was to be wrung—and now he began to see that he had all that he could ask for in the world. Yes; what was there to ask for now?

"I have nothing more for you to do," said he to the Demon; "you have done all that man could ask—you may go now."

"Go!" cried the Demon, "I shall not go until I have done all that I have to do. Give me work, or I shall wring your neck." And his fingers began to twitch.

Then the Tailor began to see into what a net he had fallen. He began to tremble like one in an ague. He turned his eyes up and down, for he did not know where to look for aid. Suddenly, as he looked out of the window, a thought struck him.

"Maybe," thought he, "I can give the Demon such a task that even he cannot do it."

"Yes, Yes!" he cried, "I have thought of something for you to do. Make me out yonder in front of my palace a lake of water a mile long and a mile wide, and let it be lined throughout with white marble, and filled with water as clear as crystal."

"It shall be done," said the Demon. As he spoke he spat in the air, and instantly a thick fog arose from the earth and hid everything from sight. Then presently from the midst of the fog there came a great noise of chipping and hammering, of digging and delving, of rushing and gurgling. All day the noise and the fog continued, and then at sunset the one ceased and the other cleared away. The poor Tailor looked out the window, and when he saw what he saw his teeth chattered in his head, for there was a lake a mile long and a mile broad, lined within with white marble, and filled with water as clear as crystal, and he knew that the Demon would come the next morning for another task to do.

That night he slept little or none, and when the seventh hour of the morning came the castle began to rock and tremble, and there stood the Demon, and his hair bristled and his eyes shone like sparks of fire. "What hast thou for me to do?" said he, and the poor Tailor could do nothing but look at him with a face as white as dough.

"What hast thou for me to do?" said the Demon again,

and then at last the Tailor found his wits and his tongue from sheer terror. "Look!" said he, "at the great mountain over yonder; remove it, and make in its place a level plain with fields and orchards and gardens." And he thought to himself when he had spoken, "Surely, even the Demon cannot do that."

"It shall be done," said the Demon, and, so saying, he stamped his heel upon the ground. Instantly the earth began to tremble and quake, and there came a great rumbling like the sound of thunder. A cloud of darkness gathered in the sky, until at last all was as black as the blackest midnight. Then came a roaring and a cracking and a crashing, such as man never heard before. All day it continued, until the time of the setting of the sun, when suddenly the uproar ceased, and the darkness cleared away; and when the Tailor looked out of the window the mountain was gone, and in its place were fields and orchards and gardens.

It was very beautiful to see, but when the Tailor beheld it his knees began to smite together, and the sweat ran down his face in streams. All that night he walked up and down and up and down, but he could not think of one other task for the Demon to do.

When the next morning came the Demon appeared like a whirlwind. His face was as black as ink and smoke, and sparks of fire flew from his nostrils.

"What have you for me to do?" cried he.

"I have nothing for you to do!" piped the poor Tailor.

"Nothing?" cried the Demon.

"Nothing."

"Then prepare to die."

"Stop!" said the Tailor, falling on his knees, "let me first see my wife."

"So be it," said the Demon, and if he had been wiser he would have said "No."

When the Tailor came to the princess, he flung himself on his face, and began to weep and wail. The princess asked him what was the matter, and at last, by dint of question, got the story from him, piece by piece. When she had it all she began laughing. "Why did you not come to me before?" said she, "instead of making all this trouble and uproar for nothing at all? I will give the Monster a task to do." She plucked a single curling hair from her head. "Here," said she, "let him take this hair and make it straight."

The Tailor was full of doubt; nevertheless, as there was nothing better to do, he took it to the Demon.

"Hast thou found me a task to do?" cried the Demon.

"Yes," said the Tailor. "It is only a little thing. Here is a hair from my wife's head; take it and make it straight."

When the Demon heard what was the task that the Tailor

had set him to do he laughed aloud; but that was because he did not know. He took the hair and stroked it between his thumb and finger, and, when he had done, it curled more than ever. Then he looked serious, and slapped it between his palms, and that did not better matters, for it curled as much as ever. Then he frowned, and began beating the hair with his palm upon his knees, and that only made it worse. All that day he labored and strove at his task, trying to make that one little hair straight, and, when the sun set, there was the hair just as crooked as ever. Then, as the great round sun sank red behind the trees, the Demon knew that he was beaten. "I am conquered! I am conquered!" he howled, and flew away, bellowing so dreadfully that all the world trembled.

So ends the story, with only this to say:

Where man's strength fails, woman's wit prevails.

·　For, to my mind, the princess—not to speak of her husband the little Tailor—did more with a single little hair and her mother wit than King Solomon with all his wisdom.

"WHOSE turn is it next to tell us a story?" said Sindbad the Sailor.

"'Twas my turn," said St. George; "but here be two ladies present, and neither hath so much as spoken a word of a story for all this time. If you, madam," said he to Cinderella, "will tell us a tale, I will gladly give up my turn to you."

The Soldier who cheated the Devil took the pipe out of his mouth and puffed away a cloud of smoke. "Aye," said he, "always remember the ladies, say I. That is a soldier's trade."

"Very well, then; if it is your pleasure," said Cinderella, "I will tell you a story, and it shall be of a friend of mine and of how she looked after her husband's luck. She was," said Cinderella, "a princess, and her father was a king."

"And what is your story about?" said Sindbad the Sailor.

"It is," said Cinderella, "about—

A PIECE OF GOOD LUCK

There were three students who were learning all that they could. The first was named Joseph, the second was named John, and the third was named Jacob Stuck. They studied seven long years under a wise master, and in that time they learned all that their master had to teach them of the wonderful things he knew. They learned all about geometry, they learned all about algebra, they learned all about astronomy, they learned all about the hidden arts, they learned all about everything, except how to mend their own hose and where to get cabbage to boil in the pot.

And now they were to go out into the world to practice what they knew. The master called the three students to him—the one named Joseph, the second named John, and the third named Jacob Stuck—and said he to them, said he: "You have studied faithfully and have learned all that I have been able to teach you, and now you shall not go out into the world with nothing at all. See; here are three glass balls, and that is one for each of you. Their like is not to be found in the four corners of the world. Carry the balls wherever you go, and when one of them drops to the ground, dig, and there you will certainly find a treasure."

So the three students went out into the wide world.

Well, they traveled on and on for day after day, each carrying his glass ball with him wherever he went. They traveled on and on for I cannot tell how long, until one day the ball that Joseph carried slipped out of his fingers and fell to the ground. "I've found a treasure!" cried Joseph, "I've found a treasure!"

The three students fell to work scratching and digging where the ball had fallen, and by-and-by they found something. It was a chest with an iron ring in the lid. It took all three of them to haul it up out of the ground, and when they did so they found it was full to the brim of silver money.

Were they happy? Well, they were happy! They danced around and around the chest, for they had never seen so much money in all their lives before. "Brothers," said Joseph, in exultation, "here is enough for all hands, and it shall be share and share alike with us, for haven't we studied seven long years together?" And so for a while they were as happy as happy could be.

But by-and-by a flock of second thoughts began to buzz in the heads of John and Jacob Stuck. "Why," said they, "as for that, to be sure, a chest of silver money is a great thing for three students to find who had nothing better than book-learning to help them along; but who knows but that there is something better even than silver money out in the wide world?" So, after all, and in spite of the chest of silver money they had found, the two of them were for going on to try their fortunes a little farther. And as for Joseph, why, after all, when he came to think of it, he was not sorry to have his chest of silver money all to himself.

So the two traveled on and on for a while, here and there and everywhere, until at last it was John's ball that slipped out of his fingers and fell to the ground. They digged where it fell, and this time it was a chest of gold money they found.

Yes; a chest of gold money! A chest of real gold money! They just stood and stared and stared, for if they had not seen it they would not have believed that such a thing could have been in the world. "Well, Jacob Stuck," said John, "it was well to travel a bit farther than poor Joseph did, was it not? What is a chest of silver money to such a treasure as this? Come, brother, here is enough to make us both rich for all the rest of our lives. We need look for nothing better than this."

But no; by-and-by Jacob Stuck began to cool down again,

and now that second thoughts were coming to him he would not even be satisfied with a half-share of a chest of gold money. No; maybe there might be something better than even a chest full of gold money to be found in the world. As for John, why, after all, he was just as well satisfied to keep his treasure for himself. So the two shook hands, and then Jacob Stuck jogged away alone, leaving John stuffing his pockets and his hat full of gold money, and I should have liked to have been there, to have had my share.

Well, Jacob Stuck jogged on and on by himself, until after a while he came to a great, wide desert, where there was not a blade or a stick to be seen far or near. He jogged on and on, and he wished he had not come there. He jogged on and on when all of a sudden the glass ball he carried slipped out of his fingers and fell to the ground.

"Aha!" said he to himself, "now maybe I shall find some great treasure compared to which even silver and gold are as nothing at all."

He digged down into the barren earth of the desert; and he digged and he digged, but neither silver nor gold did he find. He digged and digged; and by-and-by, at last, he did find something. And what was it? Why, nothing but something that looked like a piece of blue glass not a bit bigger than my thumb. "Is that all?" said Jacob Stuck. "And have I traveled all this weary way and into the blinding desert only for this? Have I passed by silver and gold enough to make me rich for all my life, only to find a little piece of blue glass?"

Jacob Stuck did not know what he had found.

I shall tell you what it was. It was a solid piece of good luck without flaw or blemish, and it was almost the only piece I ever heard tell of. Yes; that was what it was—a solid piece of good luck; and as for Jacob Stuck, why, he was not the first in the world by many and one over who has failed to know a piece of good luck when they have found it. Yes; it looked just like a piece of blue glass no bigger than my thumb, and nothing else.

"Is that all?" said Jacob Stuck. "And have I traveled all this weary way and into the blinding desert only for this? Have I passed by silver and gold enough to make me rich for all my life, only to find a little piece of blue glass?"

He looked at the bit of glass, and he turned it over and over in his hand. It was covered with dirt. Jacob Stuck blew his breath upon it, and rubbed it with his thumb.

Crack! Dong! Bang! Smash!

Upon my word, had a bolt of lightning burst at Jacob Stuck's feet—he could not have been more struck of a heap. For no sooner had he rubbed the glass with his thumb than with a noise like a clap of thunder there instantly stood before him a great, big man, dressed in clothes as red as a flame, and with eyes that shone sparks of fire. It was the Genie of Good Luck. It nearly knocked Jacob Stuck off his feet to see him there so suddenly.

"What will you have?" said the Genie. "I am the slave of good luck. Whosoever holds that piece of crystal in his hand him must I obey in whatsoever he may command."

"Do you mean that you are my servant and that I am your master?" said Jacob Stuck.

"Yes; command and I obey."

"Why, then," said Jacob Stuck, "I would like you to help me out of this desert place, if you can do so, for it is a poor spot for any soul to be."

"To hear is to obey," said the Genie, and, before Jacob Stuck knew what had happened to him, the Genie had seized him and was flying with him through the air swifter than the wind. On and on he flew, and the earth seemed to slide away beneath. On and on flew the flame-colored Genie until at last he set Jacob down in a great meadow where there was a river. Beyond the river were the white walls and grand houses of the king's town.

"Hast thou any further commands?" said the Genie.

"Tell me what you can do for me," said Jacob Stuck.

"I can do whatsoever thou mayest order me to do," said the Genie.

"Well, then," said Jacob Stuck, "I think first of all I would like to have plenty of money to spend."

"To hear is to obey," said the Genie, and, as he spoke, he reached up into the air and picked out a purse from nothing at all. "Here," said he, "is the purse of fortune; take from it all that thou needest and yet it will always be full. As long as thou hast it thou shalt never be lacking riches."

"I am very much obliged to you," said Jacob Stuck. "I've learned geometry and algebra and astronomy and the hidden arts, but I never heard tell of anything like this before."

So Jacob Stuck went into the town with all the money he could spend, and such a one is welcome anywhere. He lacked nothing that money could buy. He bought himself a fine house; he made all the friends he wanted, and more; he lived without a care, and with nothing to do but to enjoy himself. That was what a bit of good luck did for him.

Now the princess, the daughter of the king of that town, was the most beautiful in all the world, but so proud and haughty that her like was not to be found within the bounds of all the seven rivers. So proud was she and so haughty that she would neither look upon a young man nor allow any young man to look upon her. She was so particular that whenever she went out to take a ride a herald was sent through the town with a trumpet ordering that every house should be closed and that everybody should stay within doors, so that the princess should run no risk of seeing a young man, or that no young man by chance should see her.

One day the herald went through the town blowing his trumpet and calling in a great, loud voice: "Close your doors! Close your windows! Her highness, the princess, comes to ride; let no man look upon her on pain of death!"

Thereupon everybody began closing their doors and windows, and, as it was with the others, so it was with Jacob Stuck's house; it had, like all the rest, to be shut up as tight as a jug.

But Jacob Stuck was not satisfied with that; not he. He was for seeing the princess, and he was bound he would do so. So he bored a hole through the door, and when the princess came riding by he peeped out at her.

Jacob Stuck thought he had never seen anyone so beautiful in all his life. It was like the sunlight shining in his eyes, and he almost sneezed. Her cheeks were like milk and rose leaves, and her hair like fine threads of gold. She sat in a golden coach with a golden crown upon her head, and Jacob Stuck stood looking and looking until his heart melted within him like wax in the oven. Then the princess was gone, and Jacob Stuck stood there sighing and sighing.

"Oh, dear! dear!" said he, "what shall I do? For, proud as she is, I must see her again or else I will die of it."

All that day he sat sighing and thinking about the beautiful princess, until the evening had come. Then he suddenly thought of his piece of good luck. He pulled his piece of blue glass out of his pocket and breathed upon it and rubbed it with his thumb, and instantly the Genie was there.

This time Jacob Stuck was not frightened at all.

"What are thy commands, O master?" said the Genie.

"O Genie!" said Jacob Stuck, "I have seen the princess today, and it seems to me that there is nobody like her in all the world. Tell me, could you bring her here so that I might see her again?"

"Yes," said the Genie, "I could."

"Then do so," said Jacob Stuck, "and I will have you prepare a grand feast, and have musicians to play beautiful music, for I would have the princess sup with me."

"To hear is to obey," said the Genie. As he spoke he smote his hands together, and instantly there appeared twenty musicians, dressed in cloth of gold and silver. With them they brought hautboys and fiddles, big and little, and flageolets and drums and horns, and this and that to make music with. Again the Genie smote his hands together, and instantly there appeared fifty servants dressed in silks and satins and spangled with jewels, who began to spread a table with fine linen embroidered with gold, and to set plates of gold and silver upon

it. The Genie smote his hands together a third time, and in answer there came six servants. They led Jacob Stuck into another room, where there was a bath of musk and rose-water.
They bathed him in the bath and dressed him in clothes like an
emperor, and when he came out again his face shone, and he
was as handsome as a picture.

Then by-and-by he knew that the princess was coming,
for suddenly there was the sound of girls' voices singing and
the twanging of stringed instruments. The door flew open, and
in came a crowd of beautiful girls, singing and playing music,
and after them the princess herself, more beautiful than ever.
But the proud princess was frightened! Yes, she was. And well
she might be, for the Genie had flown with her through the
air from the palace, and that is enough to frighten anybody.
Jacob Stuck came to her all glittering and shining with jewels
and gold, and took her by the hand. He led her up the hall, and
as he did so the musicians struck up and began playing the
most beautiful music in the world. Then Jacob Stuck and the
princess sat down to supper and began eating and drinking,
and Jacob Stuck talked of all the sweetest things he could think
of. Thousands of wax candles made the palace bright as day,
and as the princess looked about her she thought she had
never seen anything so fine in all the world. After they had
eaten their supper and ended with a dessert of all kinds of

fruits and of sweetmeats, the door opened and there came a beautiful young serving-lad, carrying a silver tray, upon which was something wrapped in a napkin. He kneeled before Jacob Stuck and held the tray, and from the napkin Jacob Stuck took a necklace of diamonds, each stone as big as a pigeon's egg.

"This is to remind you of me," said Jacob Stuck, "when you have gone home again." And as he spoke he hung it around the princess's neck.

Just then the clock struck twelve.

Hardly had the last stroke sounded when every light was snuffed out, and all was instantly dark and still. Then, before she had time to think, the Genie of Good Luck snatched the princess up once more and flew back to the palace more swiftly than the wind. And, before the princess knew what had happened to her, there she was.

It was all so strange that the princess might have thought it was a dream, only for the necklace of diamonds, the like of which was not to be found in all the world.

The next morning there was a great buzzing in the palace, you may be sure. The princess told all about how she had been carried away during the night, and had supped in such a splendid palace, and with such a handsome man dressed like an emperor. She showed her necklace of diamonds, and the king and his prime-minister could not look at it or wonder at it enough.

The prime-minister and the king talked and talked the matter over together, and every now and then the proud princess put in a word of her own.

"Anybody," said the prime-minister, "can see with half an eye that it is all magic, or else it is a wonderful piece of good luck. Now, I'll tell you what shall be done," said he: "the princess shall keep a piece of chalk by her; and, if she is carried away again in such a fashion, she shall mark a cross with the piece of chalk on the door of the house to which she is taken. Then we shall find the rogue that is playing such a trick, and that quickly enough."

"Yes," said the king; "that is very good advice."

"I will do it," said the princess.

All that day Jacob Stuck sat thinking and thinking about the beautiful princess. He could not eat a bite, and he could hardly wait for the night to come. As soon as it had fallen, he breathed upon his piece of glass and rubbed his thumb upon it, and there stood the Genie of Good Luck.

"I'd like the princess here again," said he, "as she was last night, with feasting and drinking, such as we had before."

"To hear is to obey," said the Genie.

And as it had been the night before, so it was now. The Genie brought the princess, and she and Jacob Stuck feasted together until nearly midnight. Then, again, the door opened, and the beautiful servant-lad came with the tray and something upon it covered with a napkin. Jacob Stuck unfolded the napkin, and this time it was a cup made of a single ruby, and filled to the brim with gold money. And the wonder of the cup was this: that no matter how much money you took out of it, it was always full. "Take this," said Jacob Stuck, "to remind you of me." Then the clock struck twelve, and instantly all was darkness, and the Genie carried the princess home again.

But the princess had brought her piece of chalk with her, as the prime-minister had advised; and in some way or other she contrived, either in coming or going, to mark a cross upon the door of Jacob Stuck's house.

But, clever as she was, the Genie of Good Luck was more clever still. He saw what the princess did; and, as soon as he had carried her home, he went all through the town and marked a cross upon every door, great and small, little and big, just as the princess had done upon the door of Jacob Stuck's house, only upon the prime-minister's door he put two crosses. The next morning everybody was wondering what all the crosses on the house-doors meant, and the king and the prime-minister were no wiser than they had been before.

But the princess had brought her ruby cup with her, and she and the king could not look at it and wonder at it enough.

"Pooh!" said the prime-minister; "I tell you it is nothing

else in the world but just a piece of good luck—that is all it is. As for the rogue who is playing all these tricks, let the princess keep a pair of scissors by her, and, if she is carried away again, let her contrive to cut off a lock of his hair from over the young man's right ear. Then tomorrow we will find out who has been trimmed."

Yes, the princess would do that; so, before evening was come, she tied a pair of scissors to her belt.

Well, Jacob Stuck could hardly wait for the night to come to summon the Genie of Good Luck. "I want to sup with the princess again," said he.

"To hear is to obey," said the Genie of Good Luck; and, as soon as he had made everything ready, away he flew to fetch the princess again.

Well, they feasted and drank, and the music played, and the candles were as bright as day, and beautiful girls sang and danced, and Jacob Stuck was as happy as a king. But the princess kept her scissors by her, and, when Jacob Stuck was not looking, she contrived to snip off a lock of his hair from over his right ear, and nobody saw what was done but the Genie of Good Luck.

So it came towards midnight.

Once more the door opened, and the beautiful serving-lad came into the room, carrying the tray of silver with something upon it wrapped in a napkin. This time Jacob Stuck gave the princess an emerald ring for a keepsake, and the wonder of it was that every morning two other rings just like it would drop from it.

Then twelve o'clock sounded, the lights went out, and the Genie took the princess home again.

But the Genie had seen what the princess had done. As soon as he had taken her safe home, he struck his palms together and summoned all his companions. "Go," said he, "throughout the town and trim a lock of hair from over the right ear of every man in the whole place;" and so they did, from the king himself to the beggar-man at the gates. As for the prime-minister, the Genie himself trimmed two locks of hair from him, one from over each of his ears, so that the next morning he looked as shorn as an old sheep. In the morning all the town was in a hubbub, and everybody was wondering how all the men came to have their hair clipped as it was. But the princess had brought the lock of Jacob Stuck's hair away with her wrapped up in a piece of paper, and there it was.

As for the ring Jacob Stuck had given to her, why, the next morning there were three of them, and the king thought he had never heard tell of such a wonderful thing.

"I tell you," said the prime-minister, "there is nothing in it but a piece of good luck, and not a grain of virtue. It's just a piece of good luck—that's all it is."

"No matter," said the king; "I never saw the like of it in all my life before. And now, what are we going to do?"

The prime-minister could think of nothing.

Then the princess spoke up. "Your majesty," she said, "I can find the young man for you. Just let the herald go through the town and proclaim that I will marry the young man to whom this lock of hair belongs, and then we will find him quickly enough."

"What!" cried the prime-minister; "will, then, the princess marry a man who has nothing better than a little bit of good luck to help him along in the world?"

"Yes," said the princess, "I shall if I can find him."

So the herald was sent out around the town proclaiming that the princess would marry the man to whose head belonged the lock of hair that she had.

A lock of hair! Why, every man had lost a lock of hair! Maybe the princess could fit it on again, and then the fortune of him to whom it belonged would be made. All the men in the town crowded up to the king's palace. But all for no use, for never a one of them was fitted with his own hair.

As for Jacob Stuck, he too had heard what the herald had

proclaimed. Yes; he too had heard it, and his heart jumped and hopped within him like a young lamb in the spring-time. He knew whose hair it was the princess had. Away he went by himself, and rubbed up his piece of blue glass, and there stood the Genie.

"What are thy commands?" said he.

"I am," said Jacob Stuck, "going up to the king's palace to marry the princess, and I would have a proper escort."

"To hear is to obey," said the Genie.

He smote his hands together, and instantly there appeared a score of attendants who took Jacob Stuck, and led him into another room, and began clothing him in a suit so magnificent that it dazzled the eyes to look at it. He smote his hands together again, and out in the court-yard there appeared a troop of horsemen to escort Jacob Stuck to the palace, and they were all clad in gold-and-silver armor. He smote his hands together again, and there appeared twenty-and-one horses—twenty as black as night and one as white as milk, and it twinkled and sparkled all over with gold and jewels, and at the head of each horse of the one-and-twenty horses stood a slave clad in crimson velvet to hold the bridle. Again he smote his hands together, and there appeared in the ante-room twenty handsome young men, each with a marble bowl filled with gold money, and when Jacob Stuck came out dressed in his fine clothes there they all were.

Jacob Stuck mounted upon the horse as white as milk, the young men mounted each upon one of the black horses, the troopers in the gold-and-silver armor wheeled their horses, the trumpets blew, and away they rode—such a sight as was never seen in that town before, when they had come out into the streets. The young men with the basins scattered the gold money to the people, and a great crowd ran scrambling after, and shouted and cheered.

So Jacob Stuck rode up to the king's palace, and the king himself came out to meet him with the princess hanging on his arm.

As for the princess, she knew him the moment she laid eyes on him. She came down the steps, and set the lock of hair against his head, where she had trimmed it off the night before, and it fitted and matched exactly. "This is the young man," said she, "and I will marry him, and none other."

But the prime-minister whispered and whispered in the king's ear: "I tell you this young man is nobody at all," said he, "but just some fellow who has had a little bit of good luck."

"Pooh!" said the king, "stuff and nonsense! Just look at all the gold and jewels and horses and men. What will you do," said he to Jacob Stuck, "if I let you marry the princess?"

"I will," said Jacob Stuck, "build for her the finest palace that ever was seen in all this world."

"Very well," said the king, "yonder are those sand hills over there. You shall remove them and build your palace there. When it is finished you shall marry the princess." For if he does that, thought the king to himself, it is something better than mere good luck.

"It shall," said Jacob Stuck, "be done by tomorrow morning."

Well, all that day Jacob Stuck feasted and made merry at the king's palace, and the king wondered when he was going to begin to build his palace. But Jacob Stuck said nothing at all; he just feasted and drank and made merry. When night had come, however, it was all different. Away he went by himself, and blew his breath upon his piece of blue glass, and rubbed it with his thumb. Instantly there stood the Genie before him. "What wouldst thou have?" said he.

"I would like," said Jacob Stuck, "to have the sand hills over yonder carried away, and a palace built there of white marble and gold and silver, such as the world never saw before. And let there be gardens planted there with flowering plants and trees, and let there be fountains and marble walks. And let there be servants and attendants in the palace of all sorts and kinsmen and women. And let there be a splendid feast spread for to-morrow morning, for then I am going to marry the princess."

"To hear is to obey," said the Genie, and instantly he was gone.

All night there was from the sand hills a ceaseless sound as of thunder—a sound of banging and clapping and ham-mering and sawing and calling and shouting. All that night the sounds continued unceasingly, but at daybreak all was still, and when the sun arose there stood the most splendid palace it ever looked down upon; shining as white as snow, and blazing with gold and silver. All around it were gardens and fountains and orchards. A great highway had been built between it and the king's palace, and all along the highway a carpet of cloth of gold had been spread for the princess to walk upon.

Dear! Dear! How all the town stared with wonder when they saw such a splendid palace standing where the day before had been nothing but naked sand hills! The folk flocked in crowds to see it, and all the country about was alive with peo-ple coming and going. As for the king, he could not believe his eyes when he saw it. He stood with the princess and looked and looked. Then came Jacob Stuck. "And now," said he, "am I to marry the princess?"

"Yes," cried the king in admiration, "you are!"

So Jacob Stuck married the princess, and a splendid wedding it was. That was what a little bit of good luck did for him.

After the wedding was over, it was time to go home to the grand new palace. Then there came a great troop of horsemen with shining armor and with music, sent by the Genie to escort Jacob Stuck and the princess and the king and the prime-minister to Jacob Stuck's new palace. They rode along over the carpet of gold, and such a fine sight was never seen in that land before. As they drew near to the palace a great crowd of servants, clad in silks and satins and jewels, came out to meet them, singing and dancing and playing on harps and lutes. The king and the princess thought that they must be dreaming.

"All this is yours," said Jacob Stuck to the princess; and he was that fond of her, he would have given her still more if he could have thought of anything else.

Jacob Stuck and the princess, and the king and the prime-minister, all went into the palace, and there was a splendid feast spread in plates of pure gold and silver, and they all four sat down together.

But the prime-minister was as sour about it all as a crab-apple. All the time they were feasting he kept whispering and whispering in the king's ear. "It is all stuff and nonsense," said he, "for such a man as Jacob Stuck to do all this by himself. I tell you, it is all a piece of good luck, and not a bit of merit in it."

He whispered and whispered, until at last the king up and spoke. "Tell me, Jacob Stuck," he said, "where do you get all these fine things?"

"It all comes of a piece of good luck," said Jacob Stuck.

"That is what I told you," said the prime-minister.

"A piece of good luck!" said the king. "Where did you come across such a piece of good luck?"

"I found it," said Jacob Stuck.

"Found it!" said the king; "and have you got it with you now?"

"Yes, I have," said Jacob Stuck; "I always carry it about with me;" and he thrust his hand into his pocket and brought out his piece of blue crystal.

"That!" said the king. "Why, that is nothing but a piece of blue glass!"

"That," said Jacob Stuck, "is just what I thought till I found out better. It is no common piece of glass, I can tell you. You just breathe upon it so, and rub your thumb upon it thus, and instantly a Genie dressed in red comes to do all that he is bidden. That is how it is."

"I should like to see it," said the king.

"So you shall," said Jacob Stuck; "here it is," said he; and he reached it across the table to the prime-minister to give it to the king.

Yes, that was what he did; he gave it to the prime-minister to give it to the king. The prime-minister had been listening to all that had been said, and he knew what he was about. He took what Jacob Stuck gave him, and he had never had such a piece of luck come to him before.

And did the prime-minister give it to the king, as Jacob Stuck had intended? Not a bit of it. No sooner had he got it safe in his hand, than he blew his breath upon it and rubbed it with his thumb.

Crack! Dong! Boom! Crash!

There stood the Genie, like a flash and as red as fire. The princess screamed out and nearly fainted at the sight, and the poor king sat trembling like a rabbit.

"Whosoever possesses that piece of blue crystal," said the Genie, in a terrible voice, "him must I obey. What are thy commands?"

"Take this king," cried the prime-minister, "and take Jacob Stuck, and carry them both away into the farthest part of the desert whence the fellow came."

"To hear is to obey," said the Genie; and instantly he seized the king in one hand and Jacob Stuck in the other, and flew away with them swifter than the wind. On and on he flew, and the earth seemed to slide away beneath them like a cloud. On and on he flew until he had come to the farthest part of the desert. There he sat them both down, and it was as pretty a pickle as ever the king or Jacob Stuck had been in, in all of their lives. Then the Genie flew back again whence he had come.

There sat the poor princess crying and crying, and there sat the prime-minister trying to comfort her. "Why do you cry?" said he; "why are you afraid of me? I will do you no harm. Listen," said he; "I will use this piece of good luck in a way that Jacob Stuck would never have thought of. I will make myself king. I will, by means of it, summon a great army. I will conquer the world, and make myself emperor over all the earth. Then I will make you my queen."

But the poor princess cried and cried.

"Hast thou any further commands?" said the Genie.

"Not now," said the prime-minister; "you may go now;" and the Genie vanished like a puff of smoke.

But the princess cried and cried.

The prime-minister sat down beside her. "Why do you cry?" said he.

"Because I am afraid of you," said she.

"And why are you afraid of me?" said he.

"Because of that piece of blue glass. You will rub it

again, and then that great red monster will come again to frighten me."

"I will rub it no more," said he.

"Oh, but you will," said she; "I know you will."

"I will not," said he.

"But I can't trust you," said she, "as long as you hold it in your hand."

"Then I will lay it aside," said he, and so he did. Yes, he did; and he is not the first man who has thrown aside a piece of good luck for the sake of a pretty face. "Now are you afraid of me?" said he.

"No, I am not," said she; and she reached out her hand as though to give it to him. But, instead of doing so, she snatched up the piece of blue glass as quick as a flash.

"Now," said she, "it is my turn;" and then the prime-minister knew that his end had come.

She blew her breath upon the piece of blue glass and rubbed her thumb upon it. Instantly, as with a clap of thunder, the great red Genie stood before her, and the poor prime-minister sat shaking and trembling.

"Whosoever hath that piece of blue crystal," said the Genie, "that one must I obey. What are your orders, O princess?"

"Take this man," cried the princess, "and carry him away

into the desert where you took those other two, and bring my father and Jacob Stuck back again."

"To hear is to obey," said the Genie, and instantly he seized the prime-minister, and, in spite of the poor man's kicks and struggles, snatched him up and flew away with him swifter than the wind. On and on he flew until he had come to the farthest part of the desert, and there sat the king and Jacob Stuck still thinking about things. Down he dropped the prime-minister, up he picked the king and Jacob Stuck, and away he flew swifter than the wind. On and on he flew until he had brought the two back to the palace again; and there sat the princess waiting for them, with the piece of blue crystal in her hand.

"You have saved us!" cried the king.

"You have saved us!" cried Jacob Stuck. "Yes, you have saved us, and you have my piece of good luck into the bargain. Give it to me again."

"I will do nothing of the sort," said the princess. "If the men folk think no more of a piece of good luck than to hand it round like a bit of broken glass, it is better for the women folk to keep it for them."

And there, to my mind, she brewed good common sense, that needed no skimming to make it fit for Jacob Stuck, or for any other man, for the matter of that.

*   *   *

And now for the end of this story. Jacob Stuck lived with his princess in his fine palace as grand as a king, and when the old king died he became the king after him.

One day there came two men traveling along, and they were footsore and weary. They stopped at Jacob Stuck's palace and asked for something to eat. Jacob Stuck did not know them at first, and then he did. One was Joseph and the other was John.

This is what had happened to them:

Joseph had sat and sat where John and Jacob Stuck had left him on his box of silver money, until a band of thieves had come along and robbed him of it all. John had carried away his pockets and his hat full of gold, and had lived like a prince as long as it had lasted. Then he had gone back for more, but in the meantime some rogue had come along and had stolen it all. Yes; that was what had happened, and now they were as poor as ever.

Jacob Stuck welcomed them and brought them in and made much of them.

Well, the truth is truth, and this is it: It is better to have a little bit of good luck to help one in what one undertakes than to have a chest of silver or a chest of gold.

"AND now for your story, holy knight," said Fortunatus to St. George; "for 'twas your turn, only for this fair lady who came in before you."

"Aye, aye," said the saint; "I suppose it was, in sooth, my turn. Nevertheless, it gives me joy to follow so close so fair and lovely a lady." And as he spoke he winked one eye at Cinderella, beckoned towards her with his cup of ale, and took a deep draught to her health. "I shall tell you," said he, as soon as he had caught his breath again, "a story about an angel and a poor man who traveled with him, and all the wonderful things the poor man saw the angel do."

"That," said the Blacksmith who made Death sit in his pear-tree until the wind whistled through his ribs—"that, methinks, is a better thing to tell for a sermon than for a story."

"Whether or no that be so," said St. George, "you shall presently hear for yourselves."

He took another deep draught of ale, and then cleared his throat.

"Stop a bit, my friend," said Ali Baba. "What is your story about?"

"It is," said St. George, "about—

THE FRUIT OF HAPPINESS

Once upon a time there was a servant who served a wise man, and cooked for him his cabbage and his onions and his pot-herbs and his broth, day after day, time in and time out, for seven years.

In those years the servant was well enough contented, but no one likes to abide in the same place forever, and so one day he took it into his head that he would like to go out into the world to see what kind of a fortune a man might make there for himself. "Very well," said the wise man, the servant's master; "you have served me faithfully these seven years gone, and now that you ask leave to go you shall go. But it is little or nothing in the way of money that I can give you, and so you will have to be content with what I can afford. See, here is a little pebble, and its like is not to be found in the seven kingdoms, for whoever holds it in his mouth can hear while he does so all that the birds and the beasts say to one another. Take it—it is yours, and, if you use it wisely, it may bring you a fortune."

The servant would rather have had the money in hand than the magic pebble, but, as nothing better was to be had, he took the little stone, and, bidding his master good-bye, trudged out into the world to seek his fortune. Well, he jogged on and on, paying his way with the few pennies he had saved in his seven years of service, but for all of his traveling nothing of good happened to him until, one morning, he came to a lonely place where there stood a gallows, and there he sat him down to rest, and it is just in such an unlikely place as this that a man's best chance of fortune comes to him sometimes.

As the servant sat there, there came two ravens flying, and lit upon the cross-beam overhead. There they began talking to one another, and the servant popped the pebble into his mouth to hear what they might say.

"Yonder is a traveler in the world," said the first raven.

"Yes," said the second, "and if he only knew how to set about it, his fortune is as good as made."

"How is that so?" said the first raven.

"Why, thus," said the second. "If he only knew enough to follow yonder road over the hill, he would come by-and-by to a stone cross where two roads meet, and there he would find a man sitting. If he would ask it of him, that man would lead him to the garden where the fruit of happiness grows."

"The fruit of happiness!" said the first raven, "and of what use would the fruit of happiness be to him?"

"What use? I tell you, friend, there is no fruit in the world like that, for one has only to hold it in one's hand and wish, and whatever one asks for one shall have."

You may guess that when the servant understood the talk of the ravens he was not slow in making use of what he heard. Up he scrambled, and away he went as fast as his legs could carry him. On and on he traveled, until he came to the crossroads and the stone cross of which the raven spoke, and there, sure enough, sat the traveler. He was clad in a weather-stained coat, and he wore dusty boots, and the servant bade him good-morning.

How should the servant know that it was an angel whom he beheld, and not a common wayfarer?

"Whither away, comrade?" asked the traveler.

"Out in the world," said the servant, "to seek my fortune. And what I want to know is this—will you guide me to where I can find the fruit of happiness?"

"You ask a great thing of me," said the other; "nevertheless, since you do ask it, it is not for me to refuse, though I may tell you that many a man has sought for that fruit, and few indeed

have found it. But if I guide you to the garden where the fruit grows, there is one condition you must fulfill: many strange things will happen upon our journey between here and there, but concerning all you see you must ask not a question and say not a word. Do you agree to that?"

"Yes," said the servant, "I do."

"Very well," said his new comrade; "then let us be jogging, for I have business in the town tonight, and the time is none too long to get there."

So all the rest of that day they journeyed onward together, until, towards evening, they came to a town with high towers and steep roofs and tall spires. The servant's companion entered the gate as though he knew the place right well, and led the way up one street and down another, until, by-and-by, they came to a noble house that stood a little apart by itself, with gardens of flowers and fruit-trees all around it. There the traveling companion stopped, and, drawing out a little pipe from under his jacket, began playing so sweetly upon it that it made one's heart stand still to listen to the music.

Well, he played and played until, by-and-by, the door opened, and out came a serving-man. "Ho, piper!" said he, "would you like to earn good wages for your playing?"

"Yes," said the traveling companion, "I would, for that is why I came hither."

"Then follow me," said the servant, and thereupon the traveling companion tucked away his pipe and entered, with the other at his heels.

The house-servant led the way from one room to another, each grander than the one they left behind, until at last he came to a great hall where dozens of servants were serving a fine feast. But only one man sat at table—a young man with a face so sorrowful that it made a body's heart ache to look upon him. "Can you play good music, piper?" said he.

"Yes," said the piper, "that I can, for I know a tune that can cure sorrow. But before I blow my pipe I and my friend here must have something to eat and drink, for one cannot play well with an empty stomach."

"So be it," said the young man; "sit down with me and eat and drink."

So the two did without second bidding, and such food and drink the serving-man had never tasted in his life before. And while they were feasting together the young man told them his story, and why it was he was so sad. A year before he had married a young lady, the most beautiful in all that kingdom, and had friends and comrades and all things that a man could desire in the world. But suddenly everything went wrong; his wife and he fell out and quarreled until there was no living together, and she had to go back to her old home. Then his companions deserted him, and now he lived all alone.

"Yours is a hard case," said the traveling companion, "but it is not past curing." Thereupon he drew out his pipes and began to play, and it was such a tune as no man ever listened to before. He played and he played, and, after a while, one after another of those who listened to him began to get drowsy. First they winked, then they shut their eyes, and then they nodded until all were as dumb as logs, and as sound asleep as though they would never waken again. Only the servant and the piper stayed awake, for the music did not make them drowsy as it did the rest. Then, when all but they two were tight and fast asleep, the traveling companion arose, tucked away his pipe, and, stepping up to the young man, took from off his finger a splendid ruby ring, as red as blood and as bright as fire, and popped the same into his pocket. And all the while the serving-man stood gaping like a fish to see what his comrade was about. "Come," said the traveling companion, "it is time we were going," and off they went, shutting the door behind them.

As for the serving-man, though he remembered his promise and said nothing concerning what he had beheld, his wits buzzed in his head like a hive of bees, for he thought that of all the ugly tricks he had seen, none was more ugly than this—to bewitch the poor sorrowful young man into a sleep, and then to rob him of his ruby ring after he had fed them so well and had treated them so kindly.

But the next day they jogged on together again until by-and-by they came to a great forest. There they wandered up and down till night came upon them and found them still stumbling onward through the darkness, while the poor serving-man's flesh quaked to hear the wild beasts and the wolves growling and howling around them.

But all the while the angel—his traveling companion—said never a word; he seemed to doubt nothing nor fear nothing, but trudged straight ahead until, by-and-by, they saw a light twinkling far away, and, when they came to it, they found a gloomy stone house, as ugly as eyes ever looked upon. Up stepped the servant's comrade and knocked upon the door—rap! tap! tap! By-and-by it was opened a crack, and there stood an ugly old woman, bleary-eyed and crooked and gnarled as a winter twig. But the heart within her was good for all that. "Alas, poor folk!" she cried, "why do you come here? This is a den where lives a band of wicked thieves. Every day they go out to rob and murder poor travelers like yourselves. By-and-by they will come back, and when they find you here they will certainly kill you."

"No matter for that," said the traveling companion; "we

can go no farther tonight, so you must let us in and hide us as best you may."

And in he went, as he said, with the servant at his heels trembling like a leaf at what he had heard. The old woman gave them some bread and meat to eat, and then hid them away in the great empty meal-chest in the corner, and there they lay as still as mice.

By-and-by in came the gang of thieves with a great noise and uproar, and down they sat to their supper. The poor servant lay in the chest listening to all they said of the dreadful things they had done that day—how they had cruelly robbed and murdered poor people. Every word that they said he heard, and he trembled until his teeth chattered in his head. But all the same the robbers knew nothing of the two being there, and there they lay until near the dawning of the day. Then the traveling companion bade the servant be stirring, and up they got, and out of the chest they came, and found all the robbers sound asleep and snoring so that the dust flew.

"Stop a bit," said the angel—the traveling companion— "we must pay them for our lodging."

As he spoke he drew from his pocket the ruby ring that he had stolen from the sorrowful young man's finger, and dropped it into the cup from which the robber captain drank. Then he led the way out of the house, and, if the serving-man had wondered the day before at that which his comrade did, he wondered ten times more to see him give so beautiful a ring to such wicked and bloody thieves.

The third evening of their journey the two travelers came to a little hut, neat enough, but as poor as poverty, and there the comrade knocked upon the door and asked for lodging. In the house lived a poor man and his wife; and, though the two were as honest as the palm of your hand, and as good and kind as rain in spring-time, they could hardly scrape enough of a living to keep body and soul together. Nevertheless, they made the travelers welcome, and set before them the very best that was to be had in the house; and, after both had eaten and drunk, they showed them to bed in a corner as clean as snow, and there they slept the night through.

But the next morning, before the dawning of the day, the traveling companion was stirring again. "Come," said he; "rouse yourself, for I have a bit of work to do before I leave this place."

And strange work it was! When they had come outside of the house, he gathered together a great heap of straw and sticks of wood, and stuffed all under the corner of the house. Then he struck a light and set fire to it, and, as the two walked away through the gray dawn, all was a red blaze behind them.

Still, the servant remembered his promise to his traveling

comrade, and said never a word or asked never a question, though all that day he walked on the other side of the road, and would have nothing to say or to do with the other. But never a whit did his comrade seem to think of or to care for that. On they jogged, and, by the time evening was at hand, they had come to a neat cottage with apple and pear trees around it, all as pleasant as the eye could desire to see. In this cottage lived a widow and her only son, and they also made the travelers welcome, and set before them a good supper and showed them to a clean bed.

This time the traveling comrade did neither good nor ill to those of the house, but in the morning he told the widow whither they were going, and asked if she and her son knew the way to the garden where grew the fruit of happiness.

"Yes," said she, "that we do, for the garden is not a day's journey from here, and my son himself shall go with you to show you the way."

"That is good," said the servant's comrade, "and if he will do so I will pay him well for his trouble."

So the young man put on his hat, and took up his stick, and off went the three, up hill and down dale, until by-and-by they came over the top of the last hill, and there below them lay the garden.

And what a sight it was, with the leaves shining and

glistening like so many jewels in the sunlight! I only wish that I could tell you how beautiful that garden was. And in the middle of it grew a golden tree, and on it golden fruit. The servant, who had traveled so long and so far, could see it plainly from where he stood, and he did not need to be told that it was the fruit of happiness. But, after all, all he could do was to stand and look, for in front of them was a great raging torrent, without a bridge for a body to cross over.

"Yonder is what you seek," said the young man, pointing with his finger, "and there you can see for yourself the fruit of happiness."

The traveling companion said never a word, good or bad, but, suddenly catching the widow's son by the collar, he lifted him and flung him into the black, rushing water. Splash! went the young man, and then away he went whirling over rocks and waterfalls. "There!" cried the comrade, "that is your reward for your service!"

When the servant saw this cruel, wicked deed, he found his tongue at last, and all that he had bottled up for the seven days came frothing out of him like hot beer. Such abuse as he showered upon his traveling companion no man ever listened to before. But to all the servant said the other answered never a word until he had stopped for sheer want of breath. Then—

"Poor fool," said the traveling companion, "if you had only held your tongue a minute longer, you, too, would have had the fruit of happiness in your hand. Now it will be many a day before you have a sight of it again."

Thereupon, as he ended speaking, he struck his staff upon the ground. Instantly the earth trembled, and the sky darkened overhead until it grew as black as night. Then came a great flash of fire from up in the sky, which wrapped the traveling companion about until he was hidden from sight. Then the flaming fire flew away to heaven again, carrying him along with it. After that the sky cleared once more, and, lo and behold! the garden and the torrent and all were gone, and nothing was left but a naked plain covered over with the bones of those who had come that way before, seeking the fruit that the traveling servant had sought.

It was a long time before the servant found his way back into the world again, and the first house he came to, weak and hungry, was the widow's.

But what a change he beheld! It was a poor cottage no longer, but a splendid palace, fit for a queen to dwell in. The widow herself met him at the door, and she was dressed in clothes fit for a queen to wear, shining with gold and silver and precious stones.

The servant stood and stared like one bereft of wits. "How

comes all this change?" said he, "and how did you get all these grand things?"

"My son," said the widow woman, "has just been to the garden, and has brought home from there the fruit of happiness. Many a day did we search, but never could we find how to enter into the garden, until, the other day, an angel came and showed the way to my son, and he was able not only to gather of the fruit for himself, but to bring an apple for me also."

Then the poor traveling servant began to thump his head. He saw well enough through the millstone now, and that he, too, might have had one of the fruit if he had but held his tongue a little longer.

Yes, he saw what a fool he had made of himself, when he learned that it was an angel with whom he had been traveling the five days gone.

But, then, we are all of us like the servant for the matter of that; I, too, have traveled with an angel many a day, I dare say, and never knew it.

That night the servant lodged with the widow and her son, and the next day he started back home again upon the way he had traveled before. By evening he had reached the place where the house of the poor couple stood—the house that he had seen the angel set fire to. There he beheld masons and carpenters hard at work hacking and hewing, and building a fine new house. And there he saw the poor man himself standing by giving them orders. "How is this," said the traveling servant; "I thought that your house was burned down?"

"So it was, and that is how I came to be rich now," said the one-time poor man. "I and my wife had lived in our old house for many a long day, and never knew that a great treasure of silver and gold was hidden beneath it, until a few days ago there came an angel and burned it down over our heads, and in the morning we found the treasure. So now we are rich for as long as we may live."

The next morning the poor servant jogged along on his homeward way more sad and downcast than ever, and by evening he had come to the robbers' den in the thick woods, and there the old woman came running to the door to meet him.

"Come in!" cried she; "come in and welcome! The robbers are all dead and gone now, and I use the treasure that they left behind to entertain poor travelers like yourself. The other day there came an angel hither, and with him he brought the ring of discord that breeds spite and rage and quarrelling. He gave it to the captain of the band, and after he had gone the robbers fought for it with one another until they were all killed. So now the world is rid of them, and travelers can come and go as they please."

Back jogged the traveling servant, and the next day came to the town and to the house of the sorrowful young man. There, lo and behold! Instead of being dark and silent, as it was before, all was ablaze with light and noisy with the sound of rejoicing and merriment. There happened to be one of the household standing at the door, and he knew the servant as the companion of that one who had stolen the ruby ring. Up he came and laid hold of the servant by the collar, calling to his companions that he had caught one of the thieves. Into the house they hauled the poor servant, and into the same room where he had been before, and there sat the young man at a grand feast, with his wife and all his friends around him. But when the young man saw the poor serving-man he came to him and took him by the hand, and set him beside himself at the table. "Nobody except your comrade could be so welcome as you," said he, "and this is why. An enemy of mine one time gave me a ruby ring, and, though I knew nothing of it, it was the ring of discord that bred strife wherever it came. So, as soon as it was brought into the house, my wife and all my friends fell out with me, and we quarreled so that they all left me. But, though I knew it not at that time, your comrade was an angel, and took the ring away with him, and now I am as happy as I was sorrowful before."

By the next night the servant had come back to his home again. Rap! Tap! Tap! He knocked at the door, and the wise man that had been his master opened to him. "What do you want?" said he.

"I want to take service with you again," said the traveling servant.

"Very well," said the wise man; "come in and shut the door."

And for all I know the traveling servant is there to this day. For he is not the only one in the world who has come in sight of the fruit of happiness, and then jogged all the way back home again to cook cabbage and onions and pot-herbs, and to make broth for wiser men than himself to sup.

That is the end of this story.

"I LIKE your story, holy sir," said the Blacksmith who made Death sit in a pear tree. "Nevertheless, it hath indeed somewhat the smack of a sermon, after all. Methinks I am like my friend yonder," and he pointed with his thumb towards Fortunatus, "I like to hear a story about treasures of silver and gold, and about kings and princes —a story that turneth out well in the end, with everybody happy, and the man himself married in luck, rather than one that turneth out awry, even if it hath an angel in it."

"Well, well," said St. George, testily, "one cannot please everybody. But as for being a sermon, why, certes, my story was not that—and even if it were, it would not have hurt thee, sirrah."

"No offense," said the Blacksmith; "I meant not to speak ill of your story. Come, come, sir, will you not take a pot of ale with me?"

"Why," said St. George, somewhat mollified, "for the matter of that, I would as lief as not."

"I liked the story well enough," piped up the little Tailor who had killed seven flies at a blow. "'Twas a good enough story of its sort, but why does nobody tell a tale of good big giants, and of wild boars, and of unicorns, such as I killed in my adventures you wot of?"

Old Ali Baba had been sitting with his hands folded and his eyes closed. Now he opened them and looked at the little Tailor. "I know a story," said he, "about a Genie who was as big as a giant, and six times as powerful. And besides that," he added, "the story is all about treasures of gold, and palaces, and kings, and emperors, and what not, and about a cave such as that in which I myself found the treasure of the forty thieves."

The Blacksmith who made Death sit in the pear tree clattered the bottom of his canican against the table. "Aye, aye," said he, "that is the sort of story for me. Come, friend, let us have it."

"Stop a bit," said Fortunatus; "what is this story mostly about?"

"It is," said Ali Baba, "about two men betwixt whom there was—

NOT A PIN TO CHOOSE

Once upon a time, in a country in the far East, a merchant was traveling towards the city with three horses loaded with rich goods, and a purse containing a hundred pieces of gold money. The day was very hot, and the road dusty and dry, so that, by-and-by, when he reached a spot where a cool, clear spring of water came bubbling out from under a rock beneath the shade of a wide-spreading wayside tree, he was glad enough to stop and refresh himself with a draught of the clear coolness and rest awhile. But while he stooped to drink at the fountain the purse of gold fell from his girdle into the tall grass, and he, not seeing it, let it lie there, and went his way.

Now it chanced that two wood-choppers—the elder by name Ali, the younger Abdallah—who had been in the forest all day chopping wood, came also traveling the same way, and stopped at the same fountain to drink. There the younger of the two spied the purse lying in the grass, and picked it up. But when he opened it and found it full of gold money, he was like one bereft of wits; he flung his arms, he danced, he shouted, he laughed, he acted like a madman; for never had he seen so much wealth in all of his life before—a hundred pieces of gold money!

Now the older of the two was by nature a merry wag, and though he had never had the chance to taste of pleasure, he thought that nothing in the world could be better worth spending money for than wine and music and dancing. So, when the evening had come, he proposed that they two should go and squander it all at the Inn. But the younger fellow—Abdallah—was by nature just as thrifty as the other was spend-thrift, and would not consent to waste what he had found. Nevertheless, he was generous and open-hearted, and grudged his friend nothing; so, though he did not care for a wild life himself, he gave Ali a piece of gold to spend as he chose.

By morning every copper of what had been given to the elder wood-chopper was gone, and he had never had such a good time in his life before. All that day and for a week the head of Ali was so full of the memory of the merry night that he had enjoyed that he could think of nothing else. At last, one evening, he asked Abdallah for another piece of gold, and

Abdallah gave it to him, and by the next morning it had vanished in the same way that the other had flown. By-and-by Ali borrowed a third piece of money, and then a fourth and then a fifth, so that by the time that six months had passed and gone he had spent thirty of the hundred pieces that had been found, and in all that time Abdallah had used not so much as a pistareen.

But when Ali came for the thirty-and-first loan, Abdallah refused to let him have any more money. It was in vain that the elder begged and implored—the younger abided by what he had said.

Then Ali began to put on a threatening front. "You will not let me have the money?" he said.

"No, I will not."

"You will not?"

"No!"

"Then you shall!" cried Ali; and, so saying, caught the younger wood-chopper by the throat, and began shaking him and shouting "Help! Help! I am robbed! I am robbed!" He made such an uproar that half a hundred men, women, and children were gathered around them in less than a minute. "Here is ingratitude for you!" cried Ali. "Here is wickedness and thievery! Look at this wretch, all good men, and then turn away your eyes! For twelve years have I lived with this young man as a father might live with a son, and now how does he repay me? He has stolen all that I have in the world—a purse of seventy sequins of gold."

All this while poor Abdallah had been so amazed that he could do nothing but stand and stare like one stricken dumb; whereupon all the people, thinking him guilty, dragged him off to the judge, reviling him and heaping words of abuse upon him.

Now the judge of that town was known far and near as the "Wise Judge"; but never had he had such a knotty question as this brought up before him, for by this time Abdallah had found his speech, and swore with a great outcry that the money belonged to him.

But at last a gleam of light came to the Wise Judge in his perplexity. "Can any one tell me," said he, "which of these fellows has had money of late, and which has had none?"

His question was one easily enough answered; a score of people were there to testify that the elder of the two had been living well and spending money freely for six months and more, and a score were also there to swear that Abdallah had lived all the while in penury. "Then that decides the matter," said the Wise Judge. "The money belongs to the elder wood-chopper."

"But listen, oh my lord judge!" cried Abdallah. "All that this man has spent I have given to him—I, who found the money. Yes, my lord, I have given it to him, and myself have spent not so much as a single mite."

All who were present shouted with laughter at Abdallah's speech, for who would believe that any one would be so generous as to spend all upon another and none upon himself?

So poor Abdallah was beaten with rods until he confessed where he had hidden his money; then the Wise Judge handed fifty sequins to Ali and kept twenty himself for his decision, and all went their way praising his justice and judgment.

That is to say, all but poor Abdallah; he went to his home weeping and wailing, and with everyone pointing the finger of scorn at him. He was just as poor as ever, and his back was sore with the beating that he had suffered. All that night he continued to weep and wail, and when the morning had come he was weeping and wailing still.

Now it chanced that a wise man passed that way, and, hearing his lamentation, stopped to inquire the cause of his trouble. Abdallah told the other of his sorrow, and the wise man listened, smiling, till he was done, and then he laughed outright. "My son," said he, "if every one in your case should shed tears as abundantly as you have done, the world would have been drowned in salt water by this time. As for your friend, think not ill of him; no man loveth another who is always giving."

"Nay," said the young wood-chopper, "I believe not a word

of what you say. Had I been in his place I would have been grateful for the benefits, and not have hated the giver."

But the wise man only laughed louder than ever. "Maybe you will have the chance to prove what you say some day," said he, and went his way, still shaking with his merriment.

"All this," said Ali Baba, "is only the beginning of my story; and now if the damsel will fill up my pot of ale, I will begin in earnest and tell about the cave of the Genie."

He watched Little Brown Betty until she had filled his mug, and the froth ran over the top. Then he took a deep draught and began again.

Though Abdallah had affirmed that he did not believe what the wise man had said, nevertheless the words of the other were a comfort, for it makes one feel easier in trouble to be told that others have been in a like case with one's self.

So, by-and-by, Abdallah plucked up some spirit, and, saddling his ass and shouldering his axe, started off to the forest for a bundle of wood.

Misfortunes, they say, never come singly, and so it seemed to be with the wood-chopper that day; for that happened that had never happened to him before—he lost his way in the woods. On he went, deeper and deeper into the thickets, driving his ass before him, bewailing himself and rapping his head with his knuckles. But all his sorrowing helped him nothing, and by the time that night fell he found himself deep in the midst of a great forest full of wild beasts, the very thought of which curdled his blood. He had had nothing to eat all day long, and now the only resting-place left him was the branches of some tree. So, unsaddling his ass and leaving it to shift for itself, he climbed to and roosted himself in the crotch of a great limb.

In spite of his hunger he presently fell asleep, for trouble breeds weariness as it breeds grief.

About the dawning of the day he was awakened by the sound of voices and the glaring of lights. He craned his neck and looked down, and there he saw a sight that filled him with amazement: three old men riding each upon a milk-white horse and each bearing a lighted torch in his hand, to light the way through the dark forest.

When they had come just below where Abdallah sat, they dismounted and fastened their several horses to as many trees. Then he who rode first of the three, and who wore a red cap and who seemed to be the chief of them, walked solemnly up to a great rock that stood in the hillside, and, breaking a switch from a shrub that grew in a cleft, struck the face of the stone, crying in a loud voice, "I command thee to open, in the name of the red Aldebaran!"

Instantly, creaking and groaning, the face of the rock opened like a door, gaping blackly. Then, one after another, the three old men entered, and nothing was left but the dull light of their torches, shining on the walls of the passage-way.

What happened inside the cavern the wood-chopper could neither see nor hear, but minute after minute passed while he sat as in amazement at all that had happened. Then presently he heard a deep thundering voice and a voice as of one of the old men in answer. Then there came a sound swelling louder and louder, as though a great crowd of people were gathering together, and with the voices came the noise of the neighing of horses and the trampling of hoofs. Then at last there came pouring from out the rock a great crowd of horses laden with bales and bundles of rich stuffs and chests and caskets of gold and silver and jewels, and each horse was led by a slave clad in a dress of cloth-of-gold, sparkling and glistening with precious gems. When all these had come out from the cavern, other horses followed, upon each of which sat a beautiful damsel, more lovely than the fancy of man could picture. Beside the damsels marched a guard, each man clad in silver armor, and each bearing a drawn sword that flashed in the brightening day more keenly than the lightning. So they all came pouring forth from the cavern until it seemed as though the whole woods below were filled with the wealth and the beauty of King Solomon's day—and then, last of all, came the three old men.

"In the name of the red Aldebaran," said he who had bidden the rock to open, "I command thee to become closed." Again, creaking and groaning, the rock shut as it had opened— like a door—and the three old men, mounting their horses, led the way from the woods, the others following. The noise and confusion of the many voices shouting and calling, the trample and stamp of horses, grew fainter and fainter, until at last all was once more hushed and still, and only the woodchopper was left behind, still staring like one dumb and bereft of wits.

But so soon as he was quite sure that all were really gone, he clambered down as quickly as might be. He waited for a while to make doubly sure that no one was left behind, and then he walked straight up to the rock, just as he had seen the old man do. He plucked a switch from the bush, just as he had seen the old man pluck one, and struck the stone, just as the old man had struck it. "I command thee to open," said he, "in the name of the red Aldebaran!"

Instantly, as it had done in answer to the old man's command, there came a creaking and a groaning, and the rock

slowly opened like a door, and there was the passageway yawn-
ing before him. For a moment or two the wood-chopper hes-
itated to enter; but all was as still as death, and finally he
plucked up courage and went within.

By this time the day was brightening and the sun rising,
and by the gray light the wood-chopper could see about him
pretty clearly. Not a sign was to be seen of horses or of treasure
or of people—nothing but a square block of marble, and upon
it a black casket, and upon that again a gold ring, in which was
set a blood-red stone. Beyond these things there was nothing;
the walls were bare, the roof was bare, the floor was bare—all
was bare and naked stone.

"Well," said the wood-chopper, "as the old men have taken
everything else, I might as well take these things. The ring is
certainly worth something, and maybe I shall be able to sell the
casket for a trifle into the bargain." So he slipped the ring upon
his finger, and, taking up the casket, left the place. "I command
thee to be closed," said he, "in the name of the red Aldebaran!"
And thereupon the door closed, creaking and groaning.

After a little while he found his ass, saddled it and bridled
it, and loaded it with the bundle of wood that he had chopped
the day before, and then set off again to try to find his way out
of the thick woods. But still his luck was against him, and
the farther he wandered the deeper he found himself in the

thickets. In the meantime he was like to die of hunger, for he had not had a bite to eat for more than a whole day.

"Perhaps," said he to himself, "there may be something in the casket to stay my stomach;" and, so saying, he sat him down, unlocked the casket, and raised the lid.

Such a yell as the poor wretch uttered ears never heard before. Over he rolled upon his back and there lay staring with wide eyes, and away scampered the jackass, kicking up his heels and braying so that the leaves of the trees trembled and shook. For no sooner had he lifted the lid than out leaped a great hideous Genie, as black as a coal, with one fiery-red eye in the middle of his forehead that glared and rolled most horribly, and with his hands and feet set with claws, sharp and hooked like the talons of a hawk. Poor Abdallah the wood-chopper lay upon his back staring at the monster with a face as white as wax.

"What are thy commands?" said the Genie in a terrible voice that rumbled like the sound of thunder.

"I—I do not know," said Abdallah, trembling and shaking as with an ague. "I—I have forgotten."

"Ask what thou wilt," said the Genie, "for I must ever obey whomsoever hast the ring that thou wearest upon thy finger. Hath my lord nothing to command wherein I may serve him?"

Abdallah shook his head. "No," said he, "there is nothing—unless—unless you will bring me something to eat."

"To hear is to obey," said the Genie. "What will my lord be pleased to have?"

"Just a little bread and cheese," said Abdallah.

The Genie waved his hand, and in an instant a fine damask napkin lay spread upon the ground, and upon it a loaf of bread as white as snow and a piece of cheese such as the king would have been glad to taste. But Abdallah could do nothing but sit staring at the Genie, for the sight of the monster quite took away his appetite.

"What more can I do to serve thee?" asked the Genie.

"I think," said Abdallah, "that I could eat more comfortably if you were away."

"To hear is to obey," said the Genie. "Whither shall I go? Shall I enter the casket again?"

"I do not know," said the wood-chopper; "how did you come to be there?"

"I am a great Genie," answered the monster, "and was conjured thither by the great King Solomon, whose seal it is that thou wearest upon thy finger. For a certain fault that I committed I was confined in the box and hidden in the cavern where thou didst find me today. There I lay for thousands of years until one day three old magicians discovered the secret of where I lay hidden. It was they who only this morning compelled me to give them that vast treasure which thou sawest them take away from the cavern not long since."

"But why did they not take you and the box and the ring away also?" asked Abdallah.

"Because," answered the Genie, "they are three brothers, and neither two care to trust the other one with such power as the ring has to give, so they made a solemn compact among themselves that I should remain in the cavern, and that no one of the three should visit it without the other two in his company. Now, my lord, if it is thy will that I shall enter the casket again I must even obey thy command in that as in all things; but, if it please thee, I would fain rejoin my own kind again—they from whom I have been parted for so long. Shouldst thou permit me to do so I will still be thy slave, for thou hast only to press the red stone in the ring and repeat these words: 'By the red Aldebaran, I command thee to come,' and I will be with thee instantly. But if I have my freedom I shall serve thee from gratitude and love, and not from compulsion and with fear."

"So be it!" said Abdallah. "I have no choice in the matter, and thou mayest go whither it pleases thee."

No sooner had the words left his lips than the Genie gave a great cry of rejoicing, so piercing that it made Abdallah's flesh creep, and then, fetching the black casket a kick that sent it flying over the tree tops, vanished instantly.

"Well," quoth Abdallah, when he had caught his breath from his amazement, "these are the most wonderful things that have happened to me in all of my life." And thereupon he fell to at the bread and cheese, and ate as only a hungry man can eat. When he had finished the last crumb he wiped his mouth with the napkin, and, stretching his arms, felt within him that he was like a new man.

Nevertheless, he was still lost in the woods, and now not even with his ass for comradeship.

He had wandered for quite a little while before he bethought himself of the Genie. "What a fool am I," said he, "not to have asked him to help me while he was here." He pressed his finger upon the ring, and cried in a loud voice, "By the red Aldebaran, I command thee to come."

Instantly the Genie stood before him. "What are my lord's commands?" said he.

"I command thee," said Abdallah the wood-chopper, who was not half so frightened at the sight of the monster this time as he had been before—"I command thee to help me out of this woods."

Hardly were the words out of his mouth when the Genie snatched Abdallah up, and, flying swifter than the lightning,

set him down in the middle of the highway on the outskirts of the forest before he had fairly caught his breath.

When he did gather his wits and looked about him, he knew very well where he was, and that he was upon the road that led to the city. At the sight his heart grew light within him, and off he stepped briskly for home again.

But the sun shone hot and the way was warm and dusty, and before Abdallah had gone very far the sweat was running down his face in streams. After a while he met a rich husband-man riding easily along on an ambling nag, and when Abdallah saw him he rapped his head with his knuckles. "Why did I not think to ask the Genie for a horse?" said he. "I might just as well have ridden as to have walked, and that upon a horse a hundred times more beautiful than the one that that fellow rides."

He stepped into the thicket beside the way, where he might be out of sight, and there pressed the stone in his ring, and at his bidding the Genie stood before him.

"What are my lord's commands?" said he.

"I would like to have a noble horse to ride upon," said Abdallah—"a horse such as a king might use."

"To hear is to obey," said the Genie; and, stretching out his hand, there stood before Abdallah a magnificent Arab horse, with a saddle and bridle studded with precious stones, and with housings of gold. "Can I do aught to serve my lord further?" said the Genie.

"Not just now," said Abdallah; "if I have further use for you I will call you."

The Genie bowed his head and was gone like a flash, and Abdallah mounted his horse and rode off upon his way. But he had not gone far before he drew rein suddenly. "How foolish must I look," said he, "to be thus riding along the high-road upon this noble steed, and I myself clad in wood-chopper's rags." Thereupon he turned his horse into the thicket and again summoned the Genie. "I should like," said he, "to have a suit of clothes fit for a king to wear."

"My lord shall have that which he desires," said the Genie. He stretched out his hand, and in an instant there lay across his arm raiment such as the eyes of man never saw before—stiff with pearls, and blazing with diamonds and rubies and emeralds and sapphires. The Genie himself aided Abdallah to dress, and when he looked down he felt, for the time, quite satisfied.

He rode a little farther. Then suddenly he bethought himself, "What a silly spectacle shall I cut in the town with no money in my purse and with such fine clothes upon my back." Once more the Genie was summoned. "I should like," said the wood-chopper, "to have a box full of money."

The Genie stretched out his hand, and in it was a casket of mother-of-pearl inlaid with gold and full of money. "Has my lord any further commands for his servant?" asked he.

"No," answered Abdallah. "Stop—I have, too," he added. "Yes; I would like to have a young man to carry my money for me."

"He is here," said the Genie. And there stood a beautiful youth clad in clothes of silver tissue, and holding a milk-white horse by the bridle.

"Stay, Genie," said Abdallah. "Whilst thou art here thou mayest as well give me enough at once to last me a long time to come. Let me have eleven more caskets of money like this one, and eleven more slaves to carry the same."

"They are here," said the Genie; and as he spoke there stood eleven more youths before Abdallah, as like the first as so many pictures of the same person, and each youth bore in his hands a box like the one that the monster had given Abdallah. "Will my lord have anything further?" asked the Genie.

"Let me think," said Abdallah. "Yes; I know the town well, and that should one so rich as I ride into it without guards he would be certain to be robbed before he had traveled a hundred paces. Let me have an escort of a hundred armed men."

"It shall be done," said the Genie, and, waving his hand, the road where they stood was instantly filled with armed men, with swords and helmets gleaming and flashing in the sun, and all seated upon magnificently caparisoned horses. "Can I serve my lord further?" asked the Genie.

"No," said Abdallah the wood-chopper, in admiration, "I have nothing more to wish for in this world. Thou mayest go, Genie, and it will be long ere I will have to call thee again," and thereupon the Genie was gone like a flash.

The captain of Abdallah's troop—a bearded warrior clad in a superb suit of armor—rode up to the wood-chopper, and, leaping from his horse and bowing before him so that his forehead touched the dust, said, "Whither shall we ride, my lord?"

Abdallah smote his forehead with vexation.

"If I live a thousand years," said he, "I will never learn wisdom." Thereupon, dismounting again, he pressed the ring and summoned the Genie. "I was mistaken," said he, "as to not wanting thee so soon. I would have thee build me in the city a magnificent palace, such as man never looked upon before, and let it be full from top to bottom with rich stuffs and treasures of all sorts. And let it have gardens and fountains and terraces fitting for such a place, and let it be meetly served with slaves, both men and women, the most beautiful that are to be found in all of the world."

"Is there aught else that thou wouldst have?" asked the Genie.

The wood-chopper meditated a long time. "I can bethink myself of nothing more just now," said he.

The Genie turned to the captain of the troop and said some words to him in a strange tongue, and then in a moment was gone. The captain gave the order to march, and away they all rode with Abdallah in the midst. "Who would have thought," said he, looking around him, with the heart within him swelling with pride as though it would burst—"who would have thought that only this morning I was a poor wood-chopper, lost in the woods and half starved to death? Surely there is nothing left for me to wish for in this world!"

Abdallah was talking of something he knew nothing of.

Never before was such a sight seen in that country, as Abdallah and his troop rode through the gates and into the streets of the city. But dazzling and beautiful as were those who rode attendant upon him, Abdallah the wood-chopper surpassed them all as the moon dims the luster of the stars. The people crowded around shouting with wonder, and Abdallah, in the fullness of his delight, gave orders to the slaves who bore the caskets of money to open them and to throw the gold to the people. So, with those in the streets scrambling and fighting for the money and shouting and cheering, and others gazing down at the spectacle from the windows and the housetops, the wood-chopper and his troop rode slowly along through the town.

Now it chanced that their way led along past the royal palace, and the princess, hearing all the shouting and the hub-bub, looked over the edge of the balcony and down into the street. At the same moment Abdallah chanced to look up, and their eyes met. Thereupon the wood-chopper's heart crumbled away within him, for she was the most beautiful princess in all the world. Her eyes were as black as night, her hair like threads of fine silk, her neck like alabaster, and her lips and her cheeks as soft and as red as rose-leaves. When she saw that Abdallah was looking at her she dropped the curtain of the balcony and was gone, and the wood-chopper rode away, sighing like a furnace.

So, by-and-by, he came to his palace, which was built all of marble as white as snow, and which was surrounded with gardens, shaded by flowering trees, and cooled by the plashing of fountains. From the gateway to the door of the palace a carpet of cloth-of-gold had been spread for him to walk upon, and crowds of slaves stood waiting to receive him. But for all these glories Abdallah cared nothing; he hardly looked about him, but, going straight to his room, pressed his ring and summoned the Genie.

"What is it that my lord would have?" asked the monster.

"Oh, Genie!" said poor Abdallah, "I would have the princess for my wife, for without her I am like to die."

"My lord's commands," said the Genie, "shall be executed if I have to tear down the city to do so. But perhaps this behest is not so hard to fulfill. First of all, my lord will have to have an ambassador to send to the king."

"Very well," said Abdallah with a sigh; "let me have an ambassador or whatever may be necessary. Only make haste, Genie, in thy doings."

"I shall lose no time," said the Genie; and in a moment was gone.

The king was sitting in council with all of the greatest lords of the land gathered about him, for the Emperor of India had declared war against him, and he and they were in debate, discussing how the country was to be saved. Just then Abdallah's ambassador arrived, and when he and his train entered the council-chamber all stood up to receive him, for the least of those attendant upon him was more magnificently attired than the king himself, and was bedecked with such jewels as the royal treasury could not match.

Kneeling before the king, the ambassador touched the ground with his forehead. Then, still kneeling, he unrolled a scroll, written in letters of gold, and from it read the message asking for the princess to wife for the Lord Abdallah.

When he had ended, the king sat for a while stroking his

beard and meditating. But before he spoke the oldest lord of the council arose and said: "O sire! If this Lord Abdallah who asks for the princess for his wife can send such a magnificent company in the train of his ambassador, may it not be that he may be able also to help you in your war against the Emperor of India?"

"True!" said the king. Then turning to the ambassador: "Tell your master," said he, "that if he will furnish me with an army of one hundred thousand men, to aid me in the war against the Emperor of India, he shall have my daughter for his wife."

"Sire," said the ambassador, "I will answer now for my master, and the answer shall be this: That he will help you with an army, not of *one* hundred thousand, but of *two* hundred thousand men. And if tomorrow you will be pleased to ride forth to the plain that lieth to the south of the city, my Lord Abdallah will meet you there with his army." Then, once more bowing, he withdrew from the council-chamber, leaving all them that were there amazed at what had passed.

So the next day the king and all his court rode out to the place appointed. As they drew near they saw that the whole face of the plain was covered with a mighty host, drawn up in troops and squadrons. As the king rode towards this vast army, Abdallah met him, surrounded by his generals. He dismounted and would have kneeled, but the king would not permit him, but, raising him, kissed him upon the cheek, calling him son. Then the king and Abdallah rode down before the ranks and the whole army waved their swords, and the flashing of the sunlight on the blades was like lightning, and they shouted, and the noise was like the pealing of thunder.

Before Abdallah marched off to the wars he and the princess were married, and for a whole fortnight nothing was heard but the sound of rejoicing. The city was illuminated from end to end, and all of the fountains ran with wine instead of water. And of all those who rejoiced, none was so happy as the princess, for never had she seen one whom she thought so grand and noble and handsome as her husband. After the fortnight had passed and gone, the army marched away to the wars with Abdallah at its head.

Victory after victory followed, for in every engagement the Emperor of India's troops were driven from the field. In two months' time the war was over and Abdallah marched back again—the greatest general in the world. But it was no longer as Abdallah that he was known, but as the Emperor of

India, for the former emperor had been killed in the war, and Abdallah had set the crown upon his own head.

The little taste that he had had of conquest had given him an appetite for more, so that with the armies the Genie provided him he conquered all the neighboring countries and brought them under his rule. So he became the greatest emperor in all of the world; kings and princes kneeled before him, and he, Abdallah, the wood-chopper, looking about him, could say: "No one in all the world is so great as I!"

Could he desire anything more?

Yes; he did! He desired to be rid of the Genie!

When he thought of how all his power and might—he, the Emperor of the World—how all his riches and all his glory had come as gifts from a hideous monster with only one eye, his heart was filled with bitterness. "I cannot forget," said he to himself, "that as he has given me all these things, he may take them all away again. Suppose that I should lose my ring and that some one else should find it; who knows but that they might become as great as I, and strip me of everything, as I have stripped others. Yes; I wish he was out of the way!"

Once, when such thoughts as these were passing through his mind, he was paying a visit to his father-in-law, the king. He was walking up and down the terrace of the garden meditating on these matters, when, leaning over a wall and looking down into the street, he saw a wood-chopper—just such a wood-chopper as he himself had one time been—driving an ass—just such an ass as he had one time driven. The wood-chopper carried something under his arm, and what should it be but the very casket in which the Genie had once been imprisoned, and which he—the one-time wood-chopper—had seen the Genie kick over the tree-tops.

The sight of the casket put a sudden thought into his mind. He shouted to his attendants, and bade them haste and bring the wood-chopper to him. Off they ran, and in a little while came dragging the poor wretch, trembling and as white as death; for he thought nothing less than that his end had certainly come. As soon as those who had seized him had loosened their hold, he flung himself prostrate at the feet of the Emperor Abdallah, and there lay like one dead.

"Where didst thou get yonder casket?" asked the emperor.

"Oh, my lord!" croaked the poor wood-chopper, "I found it out yonder in the woods."

"Give it to me," said the emperor, "and my treasurer shall count thee out a thousand pieces of gold in exchange."

So soon as he had the casket safe in his hands he hurried

away to his privy chamber, and there pressed the red stone in his ring. "In the name of the red Aldebaran, I command thee to appear!" said he, and in a moment the Genie stood before him.

"What are my lord's commands?" said he.

"I would have thee enter this casket again," said the Emperor Abdallah.

"Enter the casket!" cried the Genie, aghast.

"Enter the casket."

"In what have I done anything to offend my lord?" said the Genie.

"In nothing," said the emperor; "only I would have thee enter the casket again as thou wert when I first found thee."

It was in vain that the Genie begged and implored for mercy, it was in vain that he reminded Abdallah of all that he had done to benefit him; the great emperor stood as hard as a rock—into the casket the Genie must and should go. So at last into the casket the monster went, bellowing most lamentably.

The Emperor Abdallah shut the lid of the casket, and locked it and sealed it with his seal. Then, hiding it under his cloak, he bore it out into the garden and to a deep well, and, first making sure that nobody was by to see, dropped casket and Genie and all into the water.

* * *

Now had that wise man been by—the wise man who had laughed so when the poor young wood-chopper wept and wailed at the ingratitude of his friend—the wise man who had laughed still louder when the young wood-chopper vowed that in another case he would not have been so ungrateful to one who had benefited him—how that wise man would have roared when he heard the casket plump into the waters of the well! For, upon my word of honor, betwixt Ali the wood-chopper and Abdallah the Emperor of the World there was not a pin to choose, except in degree.

OLD Ali Baba's pipe had nearly gone out, and he fell a puffing at it until the spark grew to life again, and until great clouds of smoke rolled out around his head and up through the rafters above.

"I liked thy story, friend," said old Bidpai—"I liked it mightily much. I liked more especially the way in which thy emperor got rid of his demon, or Genie."

Fortunatus took a long pull at his mug of ale. "I know not," said he, "about the demon, but there was one part that I liked much, and that was about the treasures of silver and gold and the palace that the Genie built and all the fine things that the poor wood-chopper enjoyed." Then he who had once carried the magic purse in his pocket fell a clattering with the bottom of his quart cup upon the table. "Hey! my pretty lass," cried he, "come hither and fetch me another stoup of ale."

Little Brown Betty came at his call, stumbling and tumbling into the room, just as she had stumbled and tumbled in the Mother Goose book, only this time she did not crack her crown, but gathered herself up laughing.

"You may fill my canican while you are about it," said St. George, "for, by my faith, 'tis dry work telling a story."

"And mine, too," piped the little Tailor who killed seven flies at a blow.

"And whose turn is it now to tell a story?" said Dr. Faustus.

"'Tis his," said the Lad who fiddled for the Devil, and he pointed to Hans who traded and traded until he had traded his lump of gold for an empty churn.

Hans grinned sheepishly. "Well," said he, "I never did have luck at anything, and why, then, d'ye think I should have luck at telling a story?"

"Nay, never mind that," said Aladdin, "tell thy story, friend, as best thou mayst."

"Very well," said Hans, "if ye will have it, I will tell it to you; but, after all, it is no better than my own story, and the poor man in the end gets no more than I did in my bargains."

"And what is your story about, my friend?" said Cinderella.

"'Tis," said Hans, "about how—

MUCH SHALL HAVE MORE
AND LITTLE SHALL HAVE LESS

Once upon a time there was a king who did the best he could to rule wisely and well, and to deal justly by those under him whom he had to take care of; and as he could not trust hearsay, he used every now and then to slip away out of his palace and go among his people to hear what they had to say for themselves about him and the way he ruled the land.

Well, one such day as this, when he was taking a walk, he strolled out past the walls of the town and into the green fields until he came at last to a fine big house that stood by the banks of a river, wherein lived a man and his wife who were very well to do in the world. There the king stopped for a bite of bread and a drink of fresh milk.

"I would like to ask you a question," said the king to the

rich man; "and the question is this: Why are some folk rich and some folk poor?"

"That I cannot tell you," said the good man; "only I remember my father used to say that much shall have more and little shall have less."

"Very well," said the king; "the saying has a good sound, but let us find whether or not it is really true. See; here is a purse with three hundred pieces of golden money in it. Take it and give it to the poorest man you know; in a week's time I will come again, and then you shall tell me whether it has made you or him the richer."

Now in the town there lived two beggars who were as poor as poverty itself, and the poorer of the twain was one who used to sit in rags and tatters on the church step to beg charity of the good folk who came and went. To him went the rich man, and, without so much as a good-morning, quoth he: "Here is something for you," and so saying dropped the purse of gold into the beggar's hat. Then away he went without waiting for a word of thanks.

As for the beggar, he just sat there for a while goggling and staring like one moon-struck. But at last his wits came back to him, and then away he scampered home as fast as his legs could carry him. Then he spread his money out on the table and counted it—three hundred pieces of gold money! He had

never seen such great riches in his life before. There he sat
feasting his eyes upon the treasure as though they would never
get their fill. And now what was he to do with all of it? Should
he share his fortune with his brother? Not a bit of it. To be sure,
until now they had always shared and shared alike, but here
was the first great lump of good-luck that had ever fallen in
his way, and he was not for spoiling it by cutting it in two to
give half to a poor beggar-man such as his brother. Not he; he
would hide it and keep it all for his very own.

Now, not far from where he lived, and beside the river,
stood a willow-tree, and thither the lucky beggar took his purse
of money and stuffed it into a knot-hole of a withered branch,
then went his way, certain that nobody would think of looking
for money in such a hiding-place. Then all the rest of the day
he sat thinking and thinking of the ways he would spend what
had been given him, and what he would do to get the most
good out of it. At last came evening, and his brother, who had
been begging in another part of the town, came home again.

"I nearly lost my hat today," said the second beggar so
soon as he had come into the house.

"Did you?" said the first beggar. "How was that?"

"Oh! the wind blew it off into the water, but I got it again."

"How did you get it?" said the first beggar.

"I just broke a dead branch off of the willow tree and drew my hat ashore," said the second beggar.

"A dead branch!!"

"A dead branch."

"Off of the willow tree!!"

"Off of the willow tree."

The first beggar could hardly breathe.

"And what did you do with the dead branch after that?"

"I threw it away into the water, and it floated down the river."

The beggar to whom the money had been given ran out of the house howling, and down to the river-side, thumping his head with his knuckles like one possessed. For he knew that the branch that his brother had broken off of the tree and had thrown into the water, was the very one in which he had hidden the bag of money.

Yes; and so it was.

The next morning, as the rich man took a walk down by the river, he saw a dead branch that had been washed up by the tide. "Halloo!" said he, "this will do to kindle the fire with."

So he brought it to the house, and, taking down his axe, began to split it up for kindling. The very first blow he gave, out tumbled the bag of money.

But the beggar—well, by-and-by his grieving got better of its first smart, and then he started off down the river to see if he could not find his money again. He hunted up and he hunted down, but never a whit of it did he see, and at last he stopped at the rich man's house and begged for a bite to eat and lodgings for the night. There he told all his story—how he had hidden the money that had been given him from his brother, how his brother had broken off the branch and had thrown it away, and how he had spent the whole live-long day searching for it. And to all the rich man listened and said never a word. But though he said nothing, he thought to himself, "Maybe, after all, it is not the will of Heaven that this man shall have the money. Nevertheless, I will give him another trial."

So he told the poor beggar to come in and stay for the night; and, whilst the beggar was snoring away in his bed in the garret, the rich man had his wife make two great pies, each with a fine brown crust. In the first pie he put the little bag of money; the second he filled full, of rusty nails and scraps of iron.

The next morning he called the beggar to him. "My friend," said he, "I grieve sadly for the story you told me last night. But maybe, after all, your luck is not all gone. And now, if you will choose as you should choose, you shall not go away from here comfortless. In the pantry yonder are two great pies—one is for you, and one for me. Go in and take whichever one you please."

"A pie!" thought the beggar to himself; "does the man think that a big pie will comfort me for the loss of three hundred pieces of money?" Nevertheless, as it was the best thing to be had, into the pantry the beggar went and there began to feel and weigh the pies, and the one filled with the rusty nails and scraps of iron was ever so much the fatter and the heavier.

"This is the one that I shall take," said he to the rich man, "and you may have the other." And, tucking it under his arm, off he tramped.

Well, before he got back to the town he grew hungry, and sat down by the roadside to eat his pie; and if there was ever an angry man in the world before, he was one that day—for there was his pie full of nothing but rusty nails and bits of iron.

"This is the way the rich always treat the poor," said he.

So back he went in a fume. "What did you give me a pie full of old nails for?" said he.

"You took the pie of your own choice," said the rich man; "nevertheless, I meant you no harm. Lodge with me here one night, and in the morning I will give you something better worth while, maybe."

So that night the rich man had his wife bake two loaves of bread, in one of which she hid the bag with the three hundred pieces of gold money.

"Go to the pantry," said the rich man to the beggar in the morning, "and there you will find two loaves of bread—one is for you and one for me; take whichever one you choose."

So in went the beggar, and the first loaf of bread he laid his hand upon was the one in which the money was hidden, and off he marched with it under his arm, without so much as saying thank you.

"I wonder," said he to himself, after he had jogged along awhile—"I wonder whether the rich man is up to another trick such as he played upon me yesterday?" He put the loaf of bread to his ear and shook it and shook it, and what should he hear but the chink of the money within. "Ah ha!" said he, "he has filled it with rusty nails and bits of iron again, but I will get the better of him this time."

By-and-by he met a poor woman coming home from market. "Would you like to buy a fine fresh loaf of bread?" said the beggar.

"Yes, I would," said the woman.

"Well, here is one you may have for two pennies," said the beggar.

That was cheap enough, so the woman paid him his price

and off she went with the loaf of bread under her arm, and never stopped until she had come to her home.

Now it happened that the day before this very woman had borrowed just such a loaf of bread from the rich man's wife; and so, as there was plenty in the house without it, she wrapped this loaf up in a napkin, and sent her husband back with it to where it had started from first of all.

"Well," said the rich man to his wife, "the way of Heaven is not to be changed." And so he laid the money on the shelf until he who had given it to him should come again, and thought no more of giving it to the beggar.

At the end of seven days the king called upon the rich man again, and this time he came in his own guise as a real king. "Well," said he, "is the poor man the richer for his money?"

"No," said the rich man, "he is not"; and then he told the whole story from beginning to end just as I have told it.

"Your father was right," said the king; "and what he said was very true—'Much shall have more and little shall have less.' Keep the bag of money for yourself, for there Heaven means it to stay."

And maybe there is as much truth as poetry in this story.

AND now it was the turn of the Blacksmith who had made Death sit in his pear tree until the cold wind whistled through the ribs of man's enemy. He was a big, burly man, with a bullet head, and a great thick neck, and a voice like a bull's.

"Do you mind," said he, "about how I clapped a man in the fire and cooked him to a crisp that day that St. Peter came traveling my way?"

There was a little space of silence, and then the Soldier who had cheated the Devil spoke up. "Why yes, friend," said he, "I know your story very well."

"I am not so fortunate," said old Bidpai. "I do not know your story. Tell me, friend, did you really bake a man to a crisp? And how was it then?"

"Why," said the Blacksmith, "I was trying to do what a better man than I did, and where he hit the mark I missed it by an ell. 'Twas a pretty scrape I was in that day."

"But how did it happen?" said Bidpai.

"It happened," said the Blacksmith, "just as it is going to happen in the story I am about to tell."

"And what is your story about?" said Fortunatus.

"It is," said the Blacksmith, "about—

WISDOM'S WAGES AND FOLLY'S PAY

Once upon a time there was a wise man of wise men, and a great magician to boot, and his name was Dr. Simon Agricola.

Once upon a time there was a simpleton of simpletons, and a great booby to boot, and his name was Babo.

Simon Agricola had read all the books written by man, and could do more magic than any conjurer that ever lived. But, nevertheless, he was none too well off in the world; his clothes were patched, and his shoes gaped, and that is the way with many another wise man of whom I have heard tell.

Babo gathered rushes for a chair-maker, and he also had too few of the good things to make life easy. But it is nothing out of the way for a simpleton to be in that case.

The two of them lived neighbor to neighbor, the one in

the next house to the other, and so far as the world could see there was not a pin to choose between them—only that one was called a wise man and the other a simpleton.

One day the weather was cold, and when Babo came home from gathering rushes he found no fire in the house. So off he went to his neighbor the wise man. "Will you give me a live coal to start my fire?" said he.

"Yes, I will do that," said Simon Agricola; "but how will you carry the coal home?"

"Oh!" said Babo, "I will just take it in my hand."

"In your hand?"

"In my hand."

"Can you carry a live coal in your hand?"

"Oh yes!" said Babo; "I can do that easily enough."

"Well, I should like to see you do it," said Simon Agricola.

"Then I will show you," said Babo. He spread a bed of cold, dead ashes upon his palm. "Now," said he, "I will take the ember upon that."

Agricola rolled up his eyes like a duck in a thunder-storm. "Well," said he, "I have lived more than seventy years, and have read all the books in the world; I have practiced magic and necromancy, and know all about algebra and geometry, and yet, wise as I am, I never thought of this little thing."

That is the way with your wise man.

"Pooh!" said Babo; "that is nothing. I know how to do many more tricks than that."

"Do you?" said Simon Agricola; "then listen: tomorrow I am going out into the world to make my fortune, for little or nothing is to be had in this town. If you will go along with me I will make your fortune also."

"Very well," said Babo, and the bargain was struck. So the next morning bright and early off they started upon their journey, cheek by jowl, the wise man and the simpleton, to make their fortunes in the wide world, and the two of them made a pair. On they jogged and on they jogged, and the way was none too smooth. By-and-by they came to a great field covered all over with round stones.

"Let us each take one of these," said Simon Agricola; "they will be of use by-and-by"; and, as he spoke, he picked up a great stone as big as his two fists, and dropped it into the pouch that dangled at his side.

"Not I," said Babo; "I will carry no stone with me. It is as much as my two legs can do to carry my body, let alone lugging a great stone into the bargain."

"Very well," said Agricola; "'born a fool, live a fool, die a fool.'" And on he tramped, with Babo at his heels.

At last they came to a great wide plain, where, far or near, nothing was to be seen but bare sand, without so much as a pebble or a single blade of grass, and there night caught up with them.

"Dear, dear, but I am hungry!" said Babo.

"So am I," said Simon Agricola. "Let's sit down here and eat."

So down they sat, and Simon Agricola opened his pouch and drew forth the stone.

The stone? It was a stone no longer, but a fine loaf of white bread as big as your two fists. You should have seen Babo goggle and stare! "Give me a piece of your bread, master," said he.

"Not I," said Agricola. "You might have had a dozen of the same kind, had you chosen to do as I bade you and to fetch them along with you. 'Born a fool, live a fool, die a fool,'" said he; and that was all that Babo got for his supper. As for the wise man, he finished his loaf of bread to the last crumb, and then went to sleep with a full stomach and a contented mind.

The next morning off they started again bright and early, and before long they came to just such another field of stones as they left behind them the day before.

"Come, master," said Babo, "let us each take a stone with us. We may need something more to eat before the day is over."

"No," said Simon Agricola; "we will need no stones today."

But Babo had no notion to go hungry the second time, so

he hunted around till he found a stone as big as his head. All day he carried it, first under one arm and then under the other.

The wise man stepped along briskly enough, but the sweat ran down Babo's face like drops on the window in an April shower. At last they came to a great wide plain, where neither stock nor stone was to be seen, but only a gallows-tree, upon which one poor wight hung dancing upon nothing at all, and there night caught them again.

"Aha!" said Babo to himself. "This time I shall have bread and my master none."

But listen to what happened. Up stepped the wise man to the gallows, and gave it a sharp rap with his staff. Then, lo and behold! the gallows was gone, and in its place stood a fine inn, with lights in the windows, and a landlord bowing and smiling in the doorway, and a fire roaring in the kitchen, and the smell of the good things cooking filling the air all around, so that only to sniff did one's heart good.

Poor Babo let fall the stone he had carried all day. A stone it was, and a stone he let it fall.

"'Born a fool, live a fool, die a fool,'" said Agricola. "But come in, Babo, come in; here is room enough for two." So that night Babo had a good supper and a sound sleep, and that is a cure for most of a body's troubles in this world.

The third day of their traveling they came to farms and

villages, and there Simon Agricola began to think of showing some of those tricks of magic that were to make his fortune and Babo's into the bargain.

At last they came to a blacksmith's shop, and there was the smith hard at work, dinging and donging, and making sweet music with hammer and anvil. In walked Simon Agricola and gave him good-day. He put his fingers into his purse, and brought out all the money he had in the world; it was one golden angel. "Look, friend," said he to the blacksmith; "if you will let me have your forge for one hour, I will give you this money for the use of it."

The blacksmith liked the tune of that song very well. "You may have it," said he; and he took off his leathern apron without another word, and Simon Agricola put it on in his stead.

Presently, who should come riding up to the blacksmith's shop but a rich old nobleman and three servants. The servants were hale, stout fellows, but the nobleman was as withered as a winter leaf. "Can you shoe my horse?" said he to Simon Agricola, for he took him to be the smith because of his leathern apron.

"No," said Simon Agricola; "that is not my trade: I only know how to make old people young."

"Old people young!" said the old nobleman; "can you make me young again?"

"Yes," said Simon Agricola, "I can, but I must have a thousand golden angels for doing it."

"Very well," said the old nobleman; "make me young, and you shall have them and welcome."

So Simon Agricola gave the word, and Babo blew the bellows until the fire blazed and roared. Then the doctor caught the old nobleman, and laid him upon the forge. He heaped the coals over him, and turned him this way and that, until he grew red-hot, like a piece of iron. Then he drew him forth from the fire and dipped him in the water-tank. Phizz! the water hissed, and the steam rose up in a cloud; and when Simon Agricola took the old nobleman out, lo and behold! he was as fresh and blooming and lusty as a lad of twenty.

But you should have seen how all the people stared and goggled!—Babo and the blacksmith and the nobleman's servants. The nobleman strutted up and down for a while, admiring himself, and then he got upon his horse again. "But wait," said Simon Agricola; "you forgot to pay me my thousand golden angels."

"Pooh!" said the nobleman, and off he clattered, with his servants at his heels; and that was all the good that Simon Agricola had of this trick.

But ill-luck was not done with him yet, for when the smith saw how matters had turned out, he laid hold of the doctor and would not let him go until he had paid him the golden angel he had promised for the use of the forge. The doctor pulled a sour face, but all the same he had to pay the angel. Then the smith let him go, and off he marched in a huff.

Outside of the forge was the smith's mother—a poor old creature, withered and twisted and bent as a winter twig. Babo had kept his eyes open, and had not traveled with Simon Agricola for nothing. He plucked the smith by the sleeve: "Look'ee, friend," said he, "how would you like me to make your mother, over yonder, young again?"

"I should like nothing better," said the smith.

"Very well," said Babo; "give me the golden angel that the master gave you, and I'll do the job for you."

Well, the smith paid the money, and Babo bade him blow the bellows. When the fire roared up good and hot, he caught up the old mother, and, in spite of her scratching and squalling, he laid her upon the embers. By-and-by, when he thought the right time had come, he took her out and dipped her in the tank of water; but instead of turning young, there she lay, as dumb as a fish and as black as coal.

When the blacksmith saw what Babo had done to his mother, he caught him by the collar, and fell to giving him such a dressing down as never man had before.

"Help!" bawled Babo. "Help! Murder!"

Such a hubbub had not been heard in that town for many a day. Back came Simon Agricola running, and there he saw, and took it all in in one look.

"Stop, friend," said he to the smith, "let the simpleton go; this is not past mending yet."

"Very well," said the smith; "but he must give me back my golden angel, and you must cure my mother, or else I'll have you both up before the judge."

"It shall be done," said Simon Agricola; so Babo paid back the money, and the doctor dipped the woman in the water. When he brought her out she was as well and strong as ever— but just as old as she had been before.

"Now be off for a pair of scamps, both of you," said the blacksmith; "and if you ever come this way again, I'll set all the dogs in the town upon you."

Simon Agricola said nothing until they had come out upon the highway again, and left the town well behind them; then—"'Born a fool, live a fool, die a fool!'" said he.

Babo said nothing, but he rubbed the places where the smith had dusted his coat.

The fourth day of their journey they came to a town, and here Simon Agricola was for trying his tricks of magic again. He and Babo took up their stand in the corner of the market-place, and began bawling, "Doctor Knowall! Doctor Knowall! who has come from the other end of Nowhere! He can cure any sickness or pain! He can bring you back from the gates of death! Here is Doctor Knowall! Here is Doctor Knowall!"

Now there was a very, very rich man in that town, whose daughter lay sick to death; and when the news of this great doctor was brought to his ears, he was for having him try his hand at curing the girl.

"Very well," said Simon Agricola, "I will do that, but you must pay me two thousand golden angels."

"Two thousand golden angels!" said the rich man; "that is a great deal of money, but you shall have it if only you will cure my daughter."

Simon Agricola drew a little vial from his bosom. From it he poured just six drops of yellow liquor upon the girl's tongue. Then—lo and behold! Up she sat in bed as well and strong as ever, and asked for a boiled chicken and a dumpling, by way of something to eat.

"Bless you! Bless you!" said the rich man.

"Yes, yes; blessings are very good, but I would like to have my two thousand golden angels," said Simon Agricola.

"Two thousand golden angels! I said nothing about two thousand golden angels," said the rich man; "two thousand fiddlesticks!" said he. "Pooh! Pooh! You must have been dreaming! See, here are two hundred silver pennies, and that is enough and more than enough for six drops of medicine."

"I want my two thousand golden angels," said Simon Agricola.

"You will get nothing but two hundred pennies," said the rich man.

"I won't touch one of them," said Simon Agricola, and off he marched in a huff.

But Babo had kept his eyes open. Simon Agricola had laid down the vial upon the table, and while they were saying this and that back and forth, thinking of nothing else, Babo quietly slipped it into his own pocket, without any one but himself being the wiser.

Down the stairs stumped the doctor with Babo at his heels. There stood the cook waiting for them.

"Look," said he, "my wife is sick in there; won't you cure her, too?"

"Pooh!" said Simon Agricola; and out he went, banging the door behind him.

"Look, friend," said Babo to the cook; "here I have some of the same medicine. Give me the two hundred pennies that the master would not take, and I'll cure her for you as sound as a bottle."

"Very well," said the cook, and he counted out the two hundred pennies, and Babo slipped them into his pocket. He bade the woman open her mouth, and when she had done so he poured all the stuff down her throat at once.

"Ugh!" said she, and therewith rolled up her eyes, and lay as stiff and dumb as a herring in a box.

When the cook saw what Babo had done, he snatched up the rolling-pin and made at him to pound his head to a jelly. But Babo did not wait for his coming; he jumped out of the window, and away he scampered with the cook at his heels.

Well, the upshot of the business was that Simon Agricola had to go back and bring life to the woman again, or the cook would thump him and Babo both with the rolling-pin. And, what was more, Babo had to pay back the two hundred pennies that the cook had given him for curing his wife.

The wise man made a cross upon the woman's forehead, and up she sat, as well—but no better—as before.

"And now be off," said the cook, "or I will call the servants and give you both a drubbing for a pair of scamps."

Simon Agricola said never a word until they had gotten out of the town. There his anger boiled over, like water into the fire. "Look," said he to Babo: "'Born a fool, live a fool, die a fool.' I want no more of you. Here are two roads; you take one, and I will take the other."

"What!" said Babo, "am I to travel the rest of the way alone? And then, besides, how about the fortune you promised me?"

"Never mind that," said Simon Agricola; "I have not made my own fortune yet."

"Well, at least pay me something for my wages," said Babo.

"How shall I pay you?" said Simon Agricola. "I have not a single groat in the world."

"What!" said Babo, "have you nothing to give me?"

"I can give you a piece of advice."

"Well," said Babo, "that is better than nothing, so let me have it."

"Here it is," said Simon Agricola: "'Think well! Think well—before you do what you are about to do, think well!'"

"Thank you!" said Babo; and then the one went one way, and the other the other.

(*You may go with the wise man if you choose, but I shall jog along with the simpleton.*)

After Babo had traveled for a while, he knew not whither, night caught him, and he lay down under a hedge to sleep. There he lay, and snored away like a saw-mill, for he was wearied with his long journeying.

Now it chanced that that same night two thieves had broken into a miser's house, and had stolen an iron pot full of gold money. Day broke before they reached home, so down they sat to consider the matter; and the place where they seated themselves was on the other side of the hedge where Babo lay. The older thief was for carrying the money home under his coat; the younger was for burying it until night had come again. They squabbled and bickered and argued till the noise they made wakened Babo, and he sat up. The first thing he thought of was the advice that the doctor had given him the evening before.

"'Think well!'" he bawled out; "'Think well! Before you do what you are about to do, think well!'"

When the two thieves heard Babo's piece of advice, they thought that the judge's officers were after them for sure and certain. Down they dropped the pot of money, and away they scampered as fast as their legs could carry them.

Babo heard them running, and poked his head through the hedge, and there lay the pot of gold. "Look now," said he: "this has come from the advice that was given me; no one ever gave me advice that was worth so much before." So he picked up the pot of gold, and off he marched with it.

He had not gone far before he met two of the king's officers, and you may guess how they opened their eyes when they saw him traveling along the highway with a pot full of gold money.

"Where are you going with that money?" said they.

"I don't know," said Babo.

"How did you get it?" said they.

"I got it for a piece of advice," said Babo.

For a piece of advice! No, no—the king's officers knew butter from lard, and truth from t'other thing. It was just the same in that country as it is in our town—there was nothing in the world so cheap as advice. Whoever heard of anybody giving a pot of gold and silver money for it? Without another word they marched Babo and his pot of money off to the king.

"Come," said the king, "tell me truly; where did you get the pot of money?"

Poor Babo began to whimper. "I got it for a piece of advice," said he.

"Really and truly?" said the king.

"Yes," said Babo; "really and truly."

"Humph!" said the king. "I should like to have advice that is worth as much as that. Now, how much will you sell your advice to me for?"

"How much will you give?" said Babo.

"Well," said the king, "let me have it for a day on trial, and at the end of that time I will pay you what it is worth."

"Very well," said Babo, "that is a bargain"; and so he lent the king his piece of advice for one day on trial.

Now the chief councilor and some others had laid a plot against the king's life, and that morning it had been settled that when the barber shaved him he was to cut his throat with a razor. So after the barber had lathered his face he began to whet the razor, and to whet the razor.

Just at that moment the king remembered Babo's piece of advice. "'Think well!'" said he; "'think well! Before you do what you are about to do, think well!'"

When the barber heard the words that the king said, he thought that all had been discovered. Down he fell upon his knees, and confessed everything.

That is how Babo's advice saved the king's life—you can guess whether the king thought it was worth much or little. When Babo came the next morning the king gave him ten chests full of money, and that made the simpleton richer than anybody in all that land.

He built himself a fine house, and by-and-by married the daughter of the new councilor that came after the other one's head had been chopped off for conspiring against the king's life. Besides that, he came and went about the king's castle as he pleased, and the king made much of him. Everybody bowed to him, and all were glad to stop and chat awhile with him when they met him in the street.

One morning Babo looked out of the window, and who should he see come traveling along the road but Simon Agricola himself, and he was just as poor and dusty and travel-stained as ever.

"Come in, come in!" said Babo; and you can guess how the wise man stared when he saw the simpleton living in such a fine way. But he opened his eyes wider than ever when he heard that all these good things came from the piece of advice he had given Babo that day they had parted at the cross roads.

"Aye, aye!" said he, "the luck is with you for sure and certain. But if you will pay me a thousand golden angels, I will give you something better than a piece of advice. I will teach you all the magic that is to be learned from the books."

"No," said Babo, "I am satisfied with the advice."

"Very well," said Simon Agricola, "'Born a fool, live a fool, die a fool'"; and off he went in a huff.

That is all of this tale except the tip end of it, and that I will give you now.

I have heard tell that one day the king dropped in the street the piece of advice that he had bought from Babo, and that before he found it again it had been trampled into the mud and dirt. I cannot say for certain that this is the truth, but it must have been spoiled in some way or other, for I have never heard of anybody in these days who would give even so much as a bad penny for it; and yet it is worth just as much now as it was when Babo sold it to the king.

I HAD sat listening to these jolly folk for all this time, and I had not heard old Sindbad say a word, and yet I knew very well he was full of a story, for every now and then I could see his lips move, and he would smile, and anon he would stroke his long white beard and smile again.

Everybody clapped their hands and rattled their canicans after the Blacksmith had ended his story, and methought they liked it better than almost anything that had been told. Then there was a pause, and everybody was still, and as nobody else spoke I myself ventured to break the silence. "I would like," said I (and my voice sounded thin in my own ears, as one's voice always does sound in Twilight Land), "I would like to hear our friend Sindbad the Sailor tell a story. Methinks one is fermenting in his mind."

Old Sindbad smiled until his cheeks crinkled into wrinkles.

"Aye," said everyone, "will you not tell a story?"

"To be sure I will," said Sindbad. "I will tell you a good story," said he, "and it is about—

THE ENCHANTED ISLAND

*But it is not always the lucky one that carries away
the plums; sometimes he only shakes the tree,
and the wise man pockets the fruit.*

Once upon a long, long time ago, and in a country far, far away, there lived two men in the same town and both were named Selim; one was Selim the Baker and one was Selim the Fisherman.

Selim the Baker was well off in the world, but Selim the Fisherman was only so-so. Selim the Baker always had plenty to eat and a warm corner in cold weather, but many and many a time Selim the Fisherman's stomach went empty and his teeth went chattering.

Once it happened that for time after time Selim the

Fisherman caught nothing but bad luck in his nets, and not so much as a single sprat, and he was very hungry. "Come," said he to himself, "those who have some should surely give to those who have none," and so he went to Selim the Baker. "Let me have a loaf of bread," said he, "and I will pay you for it to-morrow."

"Very well," said Selim the Baker; "I will let you have a loaf of bread, if you will give me all that you catch in your nets to-morrow."

"So be it," said Selim the Fisherman, for need drives one to hard bargains sometimes; and therewith he got his loaf of bread.

So the next day Selim the Fisherman fished and fished and fished and fished, and still he caught no more than the day before; until just at sunset he cast his net for the last time for the day, and, lo and behold! There was something heavy in it. So he dragged it ashore, and what should it be but a leaden box, sealed as tight as wax, and covered with all manner of strange letters and figures. "Here," said he, "is something to pay for my bread of yesterday, at any rate"; and as he was an honest man, off he marched with it to Selim the Baker.

They opened the box in the baker's shop, and within they found two rolls of yellow linen. In each of the rolls of linen was another little leaden box: in one was a finger-ring of gold set with a red stone, in the other was a finger-ring of iron set with nothing at all.

That was all the box held; nevertheless, that was the greatest catch that ever any fisherman made in the world; for, though Selim the one or Selim the other knew no more of the matter than the cat under the stove, the gold ring was the Ring of Luck and the iron ring was the Ring of Wisdom.

Inside of the gold ring were carved these letters: "Whosoever wears me, shall have that which all men seek—for so it is with good-luck in this world."

Inside of the iron ring were written these words: "Whosoever wears me, shall have that which few men care for—and that is the way it is with wisdom in our town."

"Well," said Selim the Baker, and he slipped the gold ring of good-luck on his finger, "I have driven a good bargain, and you have paid for your loaf of bread."

"But what will you do with the other ring?" said Selim the Fisherman.

"Oh, you may have that," said Selim the Baker.

Well, that evening, as Selim the Baker sat in front of his shop in the twilight smoking a pipe of tobacco, the ring he wore began to work. Up came a little old man with a white beard, and he was dressed all in gray from top to toe, and he wore a black velvet cap, and he carried a long staff in his hand. He stopped in front of Selim the Baker, and stood looking at him a long, long time. At last—"Is your name Selim?" said he.

"Yes," said Selim the Baker, "it is."

"And do you wear a gold ring with a red stone on your finger?"

"Yes," said Selim, "I do."

"Then come with me," said the little old man, "and I will show you the wonder of the world."

"Well," said Selim the Baker, "that will be worth the seeing, at any rate." So he emptied out his pipe of tobacco, and put on his hat and followed the way the old man led.

Up one street they went, and down another, and here and there through alleys and byways where Selim had never been before. At last they came to where a high wall ran along the narrow street, with a garden behind it, and by-and-by to an iron gate. The old man rapped upon the gate three times with his knuckles, and cried in a loud voice, "Open to Selim, who wears the Ring of Luck!"

Then instantly the gate swung open, and Selim the Baker followed the old man into the garden.

Bang! shut the gate behind him, and there he was.

There he was! And such a place he had never seen before.

Such fruit! Such flowers! Such fountains! Such summer-houses!

"This is nothing," said the old man; "this is only the beginning of wonder. Come with me."

He led the way down a long pathway between the trees, and Selim followed. By-and-by, far away, they saw the light of torches; and when they came to what they saw, lo and behold! There was the sea-shore, and a boat with four-and-twenty oarsmen, each dressed in cloth of gold and silver more splendidly than a prince. And there were four-and-twenty slaves, carrying each a torch of spice-wood, so that all the air was filled with sweet smells. The old man led the way, and Selim, following, entered the boat; and there was a seat for him made soft with satin cushions embroidered with gold and precious stones and stuffed with down, and Selim wondered whether he was not dreaming.

The oarsmen pushed off from the shore and away they rowed.

On they rowed and on they rowed for all that livelong night.

At last morning broke, and then as the sun rose Selim saw such a sight as never mortal eyes beheld before or since. It was the wonder of wonders—a great city built on an island. The island was all one mountain; and on it, one above another and another above that again, stood palaces that glistened like snow, and orchards of fruit, and gardens of flowers and green trees.

And as the boat came nearer and nearer to the city, Selim could see that all around on the house-tops and down to the water's edge were crowds and crowds of people. All were looking out towards the sea, and when they saw the boat and Selim in it, a great shout went up like the roaring of rushing waters.

"It is the King!" they cried—"it is the King! It is Selim the King!"

Then the boat landed, and there stood dozens and scores of great princes and nobles to welcome Selim when he came ashore. And there was a white horse waiting for him to ride, and its saddle and bridle were studded with diamonds and rubies and emeralds that sparkled and glistened like the stars in heaven, and Selim thought for sure he must be dreaming with his eyes open.

But he was not dreaming, for it was all as true as that eggs are eggs. So up the hill he rode, and to the grandest and the most splendid of all the splendid palaces, the princes and noblemen riding with him, and the crowd shouting as though to split their throats.

And what a palace it was!—as white as snow and painted all inside with gold and blue. All around it were gardens blooming with fruit and flowers, and the like of it mortal man never saw in the world before.

There they made a king of Selim, and put a golden crown on his head; and that is what the Ring of Good Luck can do for a baker.

But wait a bit! There was something queer about it all, and that is now to be told.

All that day was feasting and drinking and merry-making, and the twinging and twanging of music, and dancing of beautiful dancing-girls, and such things as Selim had never heard tell of in all his life before. And when night came they lit thousands and thousands of candles of perfumed wax; so that it was a hard matter to say when night began and day ended, only that the one smelled sweeter than the other.

But at last it came midnight, and then suddenly, in an instant, all the lights went out and everything was as dark as pitch—not a spark, not a glimmer anywhere. And, just as suddenly, all the sound of music and dancing and merrymaking ceased, and everybody began to wail and cry until it was enough to wring one's heart to hear. Then, in the midst of all the wailing and crying, a door was flung open, and in came six tall and terrible men, dressed all in black from top to toe, carrying each a flaming torch; and by the light of the torches King Selim saw that all—the princes, the noblemen, the dancing-girls—all lay on their faces on the floor.

The six men took King Selim—who shuddered and shook with fear—by the arms, and marched him through dark, gloomy entries and passageways, until they came at last to the very heart of the palace.

There was a great high-vaulted room all of black marble, and in the middle of it was a pedestal with seven steps, all of black marble; and on the pedestal stood a stone statue of a woman looking as natural as life, only that her eyes were shut. The statue was dressed like a queen: she wore a golden crown on her head, and upon her body hung golden robes, set with diamonds and emeralds and rubies and sapphires and pearls and all sorts of precious stones.

As for the face of the statue, white paper and black ink could not tell you how beautiful it was.

When Selim looked at it, it made his heart stand still in his breast, it was so beautiful.

The six men brought Selim up in front of the statue, and then a voice came as though from the vaulted roof: "Selim! Selim! Selim!" it said, "what art thou doing? Today is feasting and drinking and merry-making, but beware of tomorrow!"

As soon as these words were ended the six men marched King Selim back whence they had brought him; there they left him and passed out one by one as they had first come in, and the door shut to behind them.

Then in an instant the lights flashed out again, the music began to play and the people began to talk and laugh, and King Selim thought that maybe all that had just passed was only a bit of an ugly dream after all.

So that is the way King Selim the Baker began to reign, and that is the way he continued to reign. All day was feasting and drinking and making merry and music and laughing and talking. But every night at midnight the same thing happened: the lights went out, all the people began wailing and crying, and the six tall, terrible men came with flashing torches and marched King Selim away to the beautiful statue. And every night the same voice said—"Selim! Selim! Selim! What art thou doing? Today is feasting and drinking and merry-making, but beware of tomorrow!"

So things went on for a twelvemonth, and at last came the end of the year. That day and night the merry-making was merrier and wilder and madder than it had ever been before, but the great clock in the tower went on—tick, tock! tick, tock!— and by and by it came midnight. Then, as it always happened before, the lights went out, and all was as black as ink. But this time there was no wailing and crying out, but everything as silent as death; the door opened slowly, and in came, not six men as before, but nine men as silent as death, dressed all in flaming red, and the torches they carried burned as red as blood. They took

King Selim by the arms, just as the six men had done, and marched him through the same entries and passageways, and so came at last to the same vaulted room. There stood the statue, but now it was turned to flesh and blood, and the eyes were open and looking straight at Selim the Baker.

"Art thou Selim?" said she; and she pointed her finger straight at him.

"Yes, I am Selim," said he.

"And dost thou wear the gold ring with the red stone?" said she.

"Yes," said he; "I have it on my finger."

"And dost thou wear the iron ring?"

"No," said he; "I gave that to Selim the Fisherman."

The words had hardly left his lips when the statue gave a great cry and clapped her hands together. In an instant an echoing cry sounded all over the town—a shriek fit to split the ears.

The next moment there came another sound—a sound like thunder—above and below and everywhere. The earth began to shake and to rock, and the houses began to topple and fall, and the people began to scream and to yell and to shout, and the waters of the sea began to lash and to roar, and the wind began to bellow and howl. Then it was a good thing for King Selim that he wore Luck's Ring; for, though all the beautiful snow-white palace about him and above him began to crumble to pieces like slaked lime, the sticks and the stones and the beams to fall this side of him and that, he crawled out from under it without a scratch or a bruise, like a rat out of a cellar.

That is what Luck's Ring did for him.

But his troubles were not over yet; for, just as he came out from under all the ruin, the island began to sink down into the water, carrying everything along with it—that is, everything but him and one thing else. That one other thing was an empty boat, and King Selim climbed into it, and nothing else saved him from drowning. It was Luck's Ring that did that for him also.

The boat floated on and on until it came to another island that was just like the island he had left, only that there was neither tree nor blade of grass nor hide nor hair nor living thing of any kind. Nevertheless, it was an island just like the other: a high mountain and nothing else. There Selim the Baker went ashore, and there he would have starved to death only for Luck's Ring; for one day a boat came sailing by, and when poor Selim shouted, those aboard heard him and came and took him off. How they all stared to see his golden crown—for he still wore it—and his robes of silk and satin and the gold and jewels!

Before they would consent to carry him away, they made him give up all the fine things he had. Then they took him home again to the town whence he had first come, just as poor as when he had started. Back he went to his bake-shop and his ovens, and the first thing he did was to take off his gold ring and put it on the shelf.

"If that is the ring of good luck," said he, "I do not want to wear the like of it."

That is the way with mortal man: for one has to have the Ring of Wisdom as well, to turn the Ring of Luck to good account.

And now for Selim the Fisherman.

Well, thus it happened to him. For a while he carried the iron ring around in his pocket—just as so many of us do—without thinking to put it on. But one day he slipped it on his finger—and that is what we do not all of us do. After that he never took it off again, and the world went smoothly with him. He was not rich, but then he was not poor; he was not merry, neither was he sad. He always had enough and was thankful for it, for I never yet knew wisdom to go begging or crying.

So he went his way and he fished his fish, and twelve months and a week or more passed by. Then one day he went past the baker shop and there sat Selim the Baker smoking his pipe of tobacco.

"So, friend," said Selim the Fisherman, "you are back again in the old place, I see."

"Yes," said the other Selim; "awhile ago I was a king, and now I am nothing but a baker again. As for that gold ring with the red stone—they may say it is Luck's Ring if they choose, but when next I wear it may I be hanged."

Thereupon he told Selim the Fisherman the story of what had happened to him with all its ins and outs, just as I have told it to you.

"Well!" said Selim the Fisherman, "I should like to have a sight of that island myself. If you want the ring no longer, just let me have it; for maybe if I wear it something of the kind will happen to me."

"You may have it," said Selim the Baker. "Yonder it is, and you are welcome to it."

So Selim the Fisherman put on the ring, and then went his way about his own business.

That night, as he came home carrying his nets over his shoulder, whom should he meet but the little old man in gray, with the white beard and the black cap on his head and the long staff in his hand.

"Is your name Selim?" said the little man, just as he had done to Selim the Baker.

"Yes," said Selim; "it is."

"And do you wear a gold ring with a red stone?" said the little old man, just as he had said before.

"Yes," said Selim; "I do."

"Then come with me," said the little old man, "and I will show you the wonder of the world."

Selim the Fisherman remembered all that Selim the Baker had told him, and he took no two thoughts as to what to do. Down he tumbled his nets, and away he went after the other as fast as his legs could carry him. Here they went and there they went, up crooked streets and lanes and down by-ways and alley-ways, until at last they came to the same garden to which Selim the Baker had been brought. Then the old man knocked at the gate three times and cried out in a loud voice, "Open! Open! Open to Selim who wears the Ring of Luck!"

Then the gate opened, and in they went. Fine as it all was, Selim the Fisherman cared to look neither to the right nor to the left, but straight after the old man he went, until at last they came to the seaside and the boat and the four-and-twenty oarsmen dressed like princes and the slaves with the perfumed torches.

Here the old man entered the boat and Selim after him, and away they sailed.

To make a long story short, everything happened to Selim the Fisherman just as it had happened to Selim the

Baker. At dawn of day they came to the island and the city built on the mountain. And the palaces were just as white and beautiful, and the gardens and orchards just as fresh and blooming as though they had not all tumbled down and sunk under the water a week before, almost carrying poor Selim the Baker with them. There were the people dressed in silks and satins and jewels, just as Selim the Baker had found them, and they shouted and hurrahed for Selim the Fisherman just as they had shouted and hurrahed for the other. There were the princes and the nobles and the white horse, and Selim the Fisherman got on his back and rode up to the dazzling snow-white palace, and they put a crown on his head and made a king of him, just as they had made a king of Selim the Baker.

That night, at midnight, it happened just as it had happened before. Suddenly, as the hour struck, the lights all went out, and there was a moaning and a crying enough to make the heart curdle. Then the door flew open, and in came the six terrible men with torches. They led Selim the Fisherman through damp and dismal entries and passage-ways until they came to the vaulted room of black marble, and there stood the beautiful statue on its black pedestal. Then came the voice from above—"Selim! Selim! Selim!" it cried, "what art thou doing?

Today is feasting and drinking and merry-making, but beware of tomorrow!"

But Selim the Fisherman did not stand still and listen, as Selim the Baker had done. He called out, "I hear the words! I am listening! I will beware today for the sake of tomorrow!"

I do not know what I should have done had I been king of that island and had I known that in a twelve-month it would all come tumbling down about my ears and sink into the sea, maybe carry me along with it. This is what Selim the Fisherman did (but then he wore the iron Ring of Wisdom on his finger, and I never had that upon mine).

First of all, he called the wisest men of the island to him, and found from them just where the other desert island lay upon which the boat with Selim the Baker in it had drifted.

Then, when he had learned where it was to be found, he sent armies and armies of men and built on that island palaces and houses, and planted there orchards and gardens, just like the palaces and the orchards and the gardens about him—only a great deal finer. Then he sent fleets and fleets of ships, and carried everything away from the island where he lived to that other island—all the men and the women and the children; all the flocks and herds and every living thing; all the fowls and the birds and everything that wore feathers; all the gold and the silver and the jewels and the silks and the satins, and whatever was of any good or of any use; and when all these things were done, there were still two days left till the end of the year.

Upon the first of these two days he sent over the beautiful statue and had it set up in the very midst of the splendid new palace he had built.

Upon the second day he went over himself, leaving behind him nothing but the dead mountain and the rocks and the empty houses.

So came the end of the twelve months.

So came midnight.

Out went all the lights in the new palace, and everything was as silent as death and as black as ink. The door opened, and in came the nine men in red, with torches burning as red as blood. They took Selim the Fisherman by the arms and led him to the beautiful statue, and there she was with her eyes open.

"Are you Selim?" said she.

"Yes, I am Selim," said he.

"And do you wear the iron Ring of Wisdom?" said she.

"Yes, I do," said he; and so he did.

There was no roaring and thundering, there was no shaking and quaking, there was no toppling and tumbling, there was no splashing and dashing: for this island was solid rock,

and was not all enchantment and hollow inside and underneath like the other which he had left behind.

The beautiful statue smiled until the place lit up as though the sun shone. Down she came from the pedestal where she stood and kissed Selim the Fisherman on the lips.

Then instantly the lights blazed everywhere, and the people shouted and cheered, and the music played. But neither Selim the Fisherman nor the beautiful statue saw or heard anything.

"I have done all this for you!" said Selim the Fisherman.

"And I have been waiting for you a thousand years!" said the beautiful statue—only she was not a statue any longer.

After that they were married, and Selim the Fisherman and the enchanted statue became king and queen in real earnest.

I think Selim the Fisherman sent for Selim the Baker and made him rich and happy—I hope he did—I am sure he did.

So, after all, it is not always the lucky one who gathers the plums when wisdom is by to pick up what the other shakes down.

I could say more; for, O little children! Little children! There is more than meat in many an egg-shell; and many a fool tells a story that joggles a wise man's wits, and many a man dances and junkets in his fool's paradise till it comes tumbling down about his ears some day; and there are few men who are like Selim the Fisherman, who wear the Ring of Wisdom on their finger, and, alack-a-day! I am not one of them, and that is the end of this story.

OLD Bidpai nodded his head. "Aye, aye," said he, "there is a very good moral in that story, my friend. It is, as a certain philosopher said, very true, that there is more in an egg than the meat. And truly, methinks, there is more in thy story than the story of itself." He nodded his head again and stroked his beard slowly, puffing out as he did so a great reflective cloud of smoke, through which his eyes shone and twinkled mistily like stars through a cloud.

"And whose turn is it now?" said Dr. Faustus.

"Methinks 'tis mine," said Boots—he who in fairy-tale always sat in the ashes at home and yet married a princess after he had gone out into the world awhile. "My story," said he, "hath no moral, but, all the same, it is as true as that eggs hatch chickens." Then, without waiting for any one to say another word, he began it in these words. "I am going to tell you," said he, "how—

ALL THINGS ARE AS FATE WILLS

Once upon a time, in the old, old days, there lived a king who had a head upon his shoulders wiser than other folk, and this was why: though he was richer and wiser and greater than most kings, and had all that he wanted and more into the bargain, he was so afraid of becoming proud of his own prosperity that he had these words written in letters of gold upon the walls of each and every room in his palace:

All Things are as Fate wills.

Now, by-and-by and after a while the king died; for when his time comes, even the rich and the wise man must die, as well as the poor and the simple man. So the king's son came, in turn, to be king of that land; and, though he was not so bad as the world of men goes, he was not the man that his father was, as this story will show you.

One day, as he sat with his chief councilor, his eyes fell upon the words written in letters of gold upon the wall—the words that his father had written there in time gone by:

All Things are as Fate wills;

and the young king did not like the taste of them, for he was very proud of his own greatness. "That is not so," said he, pointing to the words on the wall. "Let them be painted out, and these words written in their place:

All Things are as Man does."

Now, the chief councilor was a grave old man, and had been councilor to the young king's father. "Do not be too hasty, my lord king," said he. "Try first the truth of your own words before you wipe out those that your father has written."

"Very well," said the young king, "so be it. I will approve the truth of my words. Bring me hither some beggar from the town whom Fate has made poor, and I will make him rich. So I will show you that his life shall be as I will, and not as Fate wills."

Now, in that town there was a poor beggar-man who used to sit every day beside the town gate, begging for something for charity's sake. Sometimes people gave him a penny or two, but it was little or nothing that he got, for Fate was against him.

The same day that the king and the chief councilor had had their talk together, as the beggar sat holding up his wooden bowl and asking charity of those who passed by, there suddenly came three men who, without saying a word, clapped hold of him and marched him off.

It was in vain that the beggar talked and questioned—in vain that he begged and besought them to let him go. Not a word did they say to him, either of good or bad. At last they came to a gate that led through a high wall and into a garden, and there the three stopped, and one of them knocked upon the gate. In answer to his knocking it flew open. He thrust the beggar into the garden neck and crop, and then the gate was banged to again.

But what a sight it was the beggar saw before his eyes! flowers, and fruit trees, and marble walks, and a great fountain that shot up a jet of water as white as snow. But he had not long to stand gaping and staring around him, for in the garden were a great number of people, who came hurrying to him, and who, without speaking a word to him or answering a single question, or as much as giving him time to think, led him to a marble bath of tepid water. There he was stripped of his tattered clothes and washed as clean as snow. Then, as some of the attendants dried him with fine linen towels, others came carrying clothes fit for a prince to wear, and clad the beggar in them from head to foot. After that, still without saying a word, they let him out from the bath again, and there he found still other attendants waiting for him—two of them holding a milk-white horse, saddled and bridled, and fit for an emperor to ride. These helped him to mount, and then, leaping into their own saddles, rode away with the beggar in their midst.

They rode out of the garden and into the streets, and on and on they went until they came to the king's palace, and there they stopped. Courtiers and noblemen and great lords were waiting for their coming, some of whom helped him to dismount from the horse, for by this time the beggar was so overcome with wonder that he stared like one moon-struck, and as though his wits were addled. Then, leading the way up the palace steps, they conducted him from room to room, until at last they came to one more grand and splendid than all the rest, and there sat the king himself waiting for the beggar's coming.

The beggar would have flung himself at the king's feet, but the king would not let him; for he came down from the throne where he sat, and, taking the beggar by the hand, led him up and sat him alongside of him. Then the king gave orders to the attendants who stood about, and a feast was served in plates of solid gold upon a table-cloth of silver—a feast such as the beggar had never dreamed of, and the poor man ate as he had never eaten in his life before.

All the while that the king and the beggar were eating, musicians played sweet music and dancers danced and singers sang.

Then when the feast was over there came ten young men, bringing flasks and flagons of all kinds, full of the best wine in the world; and the beggar drank as he had never drank in his life before, and until his head spun like a top.

So the king and the beggar feasted and made merry, until at last the clock struck twelve and the king arose from his seat. "My friend," said he to the beggar, "all these things have been done to show you that Luck and Fate, which have been against you for all these years, are now for you. Hereafter, instead of being poor you shall be the richest of the rich, for I will give you the greatest thing that I have in my treasury." Then he called the chief treasurer, who came forward with a golden tray in his hand. Upon the tray was a purse of silk. "See," said the king, "here is a purse, and in the purse are one hundred pieces of gold money. But though that much may seem great to you, it is but little of the true value of the purse. Its virtue lies in this: that however much you may take from it, there will always be one hundred pieces of gold money left in it. Now go; and while you are enjoying the riches which I give you, I have only to ask you to remember these are not the gifts of Fate, but of a mortal man."

But all the while he was talking the beggar's head was spinning and spinning, and buzzing and buzzing, so that he hardly heard a word of what the king said.

Then when the king had ended his speech, the lords and gentlemen who had brought the beggar in led him forth again. Out they went through room after room—out through the court-yard, out through the gate.

Bang!—it was shut to behind him, and he found himself standing in the darkness of midnight, with the splendid clothes upon his back, and the magic purse with its hundred pieces of gold money in his pocket.

He stood looking about himself for a while, and then off he started homeward, staggering and stumbling and shuffling, for the wine that he had drank made him so light-headed that all the world spun topsy-turvy around him.

His way led along by the river, and on he went stumbling and staggering. All of a sudden—plump! splash!—he was in the water over head and ears. Up he came, spitting out the water and shouting for help, splashing and sputtering, and kicking and swimming, knowing no more where he was than the man in the moon. Sometimes his head was under water and sometimes it was up again.

At last, just as his strength was failing him, his feet struck the bottom, and he crawled up on the shore more dead than alive. Then, through fear and cold and wet, he swooned away, and lay for a long time for all the world as though he were dead.

Now, it chanced that two fishermen were out with their nets that night, and Luck or Fate led them by the way where the beggar lay on the shore. "Halloa!" said one of the fishermen, "here is a poor body drowned!" They turned him over, and then they saw what rich clothes he wore, and felt that he had a purse in his pocket.

"Come," said the second fisherman, "he is dead, whoever he is. His fine clothes and his purse of money can do him no good now, and we might as well have them as anybody else." So between them both they stripped the beggar of all that the king had given him, and left him lying on the beach.

At daybreak the beggar awoke from his swoon, and there he found himself lying without a stitch to his back, and half dead with the cold and the water he had swallowed. Then, fearing lest somebody might see him, he crawled away into the rushes that grew beside the river, there to hide himself until night should come again.

But as he went, crawling upon hands and knees, he suddenly came upon a bundle that had been washed up by the water, and when he laid eyes upon it his heart leaped within him, for what should that bundle be but the patches and tatters which he had worn the day before, and which the attendants had thrown over the garden wall and into the river when they had dressed him in the fine clothes the king gave him.

He spread his clothes out in the sun until they were dry, and then he put them on and went back into the town again.

"Well," said the king, that morning, to his chief councilor, "what do you think now? Am I not greater than Fate? Did I not make the beggar rich? And shall I not paint my father's words out from the wall, and put my own there instead?"

"I do not know," said the councilor, shaking his head. "Let us first see what has become of the beggar."

"So be it," said the king; and he and the councilor set off to see whether the beggar had done as he ought to do with the good things that the king had given him. So they came to the town-gate, and there, lo and behold! The first thing that they saw was the beggar with his wooden bowl in his hand asking those who passed by for a stray penny or two.

When the king saw him he turned without a word, and rode back home again. "Very well," said he to the chief councilor, "I have tried to make the beggar rich and have failed; nevertheless, if I cannot make him I can ruin him in spite of Fate, and that I will show you."

So all that while the beggar sat at the town-gate and begged until came noontide, when who should he see coming but the same three men who had come for him the day before. "Ah, ha!" said he to himself, "now the king is going to give me some more good things." And so when the three reached him he was willing enough to go with them, rough as they were.

Off they marched; but this time they did not come to any garden with fruits and flowers and fountains and marble baths. Off they marched, and when they stopped it was in front of the king's palace. This time no nobles and great lords and courtiers were waiting for his coming; but instead of that the town hangman—a great ugly fellow, clad in black from head to foot. Up he came to the beggar, and, catching him by the scruff of the neck, dragged him up the palace steps and from room to room until at last he flung him down at the king's feet.

When the poor beggar gathered wits enough to look about him he saw there a great chest standing wide open, and with holes in the lid. He wondered what it was for, but the king gave him no chance to ask; for, beckoning with his hand, the hangman and the others caught the beggar by arms and legs, thrust him into the chest, and banged down the lid upon him.

The king locked it and double-locked it, and set his seal upon it; and there was the beggar as tight as a fly in a bottle.

They carried the chest out and thrust it into a cart and hauled it away, until at last they came to the sea-shore. There they flung chest and all into the water, and it floated away like a cork. And that is how the king set about to ruin the poor beggar-man.

Well, the chest floated on and on for three days, and then at last it came to the shore of a country far away. There the waves caught it up, and flung it so hard upon the rocks of the sea-beach that the chest was burst open by the blow, and the beggar crawled out with eyes as big as saucers and face as white as dough. After he had sat for a while, and when his wits came back to him and he had gathered strength enough, he stood up and looked around to see where Fate had cast him; and far away on the hill-side he saw the walls and the roofs and the towers of the great town, shining in the sunlight as white as snow.

"Well," said he, "here is something to be thankful for, at least," and so saying and shaking the stiffness out of his knees and elbows, he started off for the white walls and the red roofs in the distance.

At last he reached the great gate, and through it he could see the stony streets and multitudes of people coming and going.

But it was not for him to enter that gate. Out popped two soldiers with great battle-axes in their hands and looking as fierce as dragons. "Are you a stranger in this town?" said one in a great, gruff voice.

"Yes," said the beggar, "I am."

"And where are you going?"

"I am going into the town."

"No, you are not."

"Why not?"

"Because no stranger enters here. Yonder is the pathway. You must take that if you would enter the town."

"Very well," said the beggar, "I would just as lief go into the town that way as another."

So off he marched without another word. On and on he went along the narrow pathway until at last he came to a little gate of polished brass. Over the gate were written these words, in great letters as red as blood:

"Who Enters here Shall Surely Die."

Many and many a man besides the beggar had traveled that path and looked up at those letters, and when he had read

them had turned and gone away again. But the beggar neither turned nor went away; because why, he could neither read nor write a word, and so the blood-red letters had no fear for him. Up he marched to the brazen gate, as boldly as though it had been a kitchen door, and—Rap! Tap! Tap! He knocked upon it. He waited awhile, but nobody came. Rap! Tap! Tap! He knocked again; and then, after a little while, for the third time—Rap! Tap! Tap! Then instantly the gate swung open and he entered. So soon as he had crossed the threshold it was banged to behind him again, just as the garden gate had been when the king had first sent for him. He found himself in a long, dark entry, and at the end of it another door, and over it the same words, written in blood-red letters:

"Beware! Beware! Who Enters here Shall Surely Die!"

"Well," said the beggar, "this is the hardest town for a body to come into that I ever saw." And then he opened the second door and passed through.

It was fit to deafen a body! Such a shout the beggar's ears had never heard before; such a sight the beggar's eyes had never beheld, for there, before him, was a great splendid hall of marble as white as snow. All along the hall stood scores of lords and ladies in silks and satins, and with jewels on their necks and arms fit to dazzle a body's eyes. Right up the middle of the hall stretched a carpet of blue velvet, and at the farther end, on a throne of gold, sat a lady as beautiful as the sun and moon and all the stars.

"Welcome! welcome!" they all shouted, until the beggar was nearly deafened by the noise they all made, and the lady herself stood up and smiled upon him.

Then there came three young men, and led the beggar up the carpet of velvet to the throne of gold.

"Welcome, my hero!" said the beautiful lady; "and have you, then, come at last?"

"Yes," said the beggar, "I have."

"Long have I waited for you," said the lady; "long have I waited for the hero who would dare without fear to come through the two gates of death to marry me and to rule as king over this country, and now at last you are here."

"Yes," said the beggar, "I am."

Meanwhile, while all these things were happening, the king of that other country had painted out the words his father had written on the walls, and had had these words painted in in their stead:

"All Things are as Man does."

For a while he was very well satisfied with them, until, a week after, he was bidden to the wedding of the Queen of the Golden Mountains; for when he came there who should the bridegroom be but the beggar whom he had set adrift in the wooden box a week or so before.

The bridegroom winked at him, but said never a word, good or ill, for he was willing to let all that had happened be past and gone. But the king saw how matters stood as clear as daylight, and when he got back home again he had the new words that stood on the walls of the room painted out, and had the old ones painted in in bigger letters than ever:

"All Things are as Fate wills."

ALL the good people who were gathered around the table of the Sign of Mother Goose sat thinking for a while over the story. As for Boots, he buried his face in the quart pot and took a long, long pull at the ale.

"Methinks," said the Soldier who cheated the Devil, presently breaking silence—"methinks there be very few of the women folk who do their share of this story-telling. So far we have had but one, and that is Lady Cinderella. I see another one present, and drink to her health."

He winked his eye at Patient Grizzle, beckoning towards her with his quart pot, and took a long and hearty pull. Then he banged his mug down upon the table. "Fetch me another glass, lass," said he to Little Brown Betty. "Meantime, fair lady"—this he said to Patient Grizzle—"will you not entertain us with some story of your own?"

"I know not," said Patient Grizzle, "that I can tell you any story worth your hearing."

"Aye, aye, but you can," said the Soldier who cheated the Devil; "and, moreover, anything coming from betwixt such red lips and such white teeth will be worth the listening to."

Patient Grizzle smiled, and the brave little Tailor, and the

Lad who fiddled for the Devil, and Hans and Bidpai and Boots nodded approval.

"Aye," said Ali Baba, "it is true enough that there have been but few of the women folk who have had their say, and methinks that it is very strange and unaccountable, for nearly always they have plenty to speak in their own behalf."

All who sat there in Twilight Land laughed, and even Patient Grizzle smiled.

"Very well," said Patient Grizzle, "if you will have it, I will tell you a story. It is about a fisherman who was married and had a wife of his own, and who made her carry all the load of everything that happened to him. For he, like most men I wot of, had found out—

WHERE TO LAY THE BLAME

*M*any and many a man has come to trouble—so he will say—
by following his wife's advice. This is how it was with a man of
whom I shall tell you.

There was once upon a time a fisherman who had fished
all day long and had caught not so much as a sprat. So at night
there he sat by the fire, rubbing his knees and warming his
shins, and waiting for supper that his wife was cooking for
him, and his hunger was as sharp as vinegar, and his temper
hot enough to fry fat.

While he sat there grumbling and growling and trying to
make himself comfortable and warm, there suddenly came a
knock at the door. The good woman opened it, and there stood
an old man, clad all in red from head to foot, and with a snowy
beard at his chin as white as winter snow.

The fisherman's wife stood gaping and staring at the strange figure, but the old man in red walked straight into the hut. "Bring your nets, fisherman," said he, "and come with me. There is something that I want you to catch for me, and if I have luck I will pay you for your fishing as never fisherman was paid before."

"Not I," said the fisherman; "I go out no more this night. I have been fishing all day long until my back is nearly broken, and have caught nothing, and now I am not such a fool as to go out and leave a warm fire and a good supper at your bidding."

But the fisherman's wife had listened to what the old man had said about paying for the job, and she was of a different mind from her husband. "Come," said she, "the old man promises to pay you well. This is not a chance to be lost, I can tell you, and my advice to you is that you go."

The fisherman shook his head. No, he would not go; he had said he would not, and he would not. But the wife only smiled and said again, "My advice to you is that you go."

The fisherman grumbled and grumbled, and swore that he would not go. The wife said nothing but one thing. She did not argue; she did not lose her temper; she only said to everything that he said, "My advice to you is that you go."

At last the fisherman's anger boiled over. "Very well," said he, spitting his words at her; "if you will drive me out into the night, I suppose I will have to go."

Then down he took his fur cap and up he took his nets, and off he and the old man marched through the moonlight, their shadows bobbing along like black spiders behind them.

Well, on they went, out from the town and across the fields and through the woods, until at last they came to a dreary, lonesome desert, where nothing was to be seen but gray rocks and weeds and thistles.

"Well," said the fisherman, "I have fished, man and boy, for forty-seven years, but never did I see as unlikely a place to catch anything as this."

But the old man said never a word. First of all he drew a great circle with strange figures, marking it with his finger upon the ground. Then out from under his red gown he brought a tinder-box and steel, and a little silver casket covered all over with strange figures of serpents and dragons and what not. He brought some sticks of spice-wood from his pouch, and then he struck a light and made a fire. Out of the box he took a gray powder, which he flung upon the little blaze.

Puff! Flash! A vivid flame went up into the moonlight, and then a dense smoke as black as ink, which spread out wider and wider, far and near, till all below was darker than the darkest midnight. Then the old man began to utter strange spells and words. Presently there began a rumbling that sounded louder and louder and nearer and nearer, until it roared and bellowed like thunder. The earth rocked and swayed, and the poor fisherman shook and trembled with fear till his teeth clattered in his head.

Then suddenly the roaring and bellowing ceased, and all was as still as death, though the darkness was as thick and black as ever.

"Now," said the old magician—for such he was—"now we are about to take a journey such as no one ever traveled before. Heed well what I tell you. Speak not a single word, for if you do, misfortune will be sure to happen."

"Ain't I to say anything?" said the fisherman.

"No."

"Not even 'boo' to a goose?"

"No."

"Well, that is pretty hard upon a man who likes to say his say," said the fisherman.

"And moreover," said the old man, "I must blindfold you as well."

Thereupon he took from his pocket a handkerchief, and made ready to tie it about the fisherman's eyes.

"And ain't I to see anything at all?" said the fisherman.

"No."

"Not even so much as a single feather?"

"No."

"Well, then," said the fisherman, "I wish I'd not come."

But the old man tied the handkerchief tightly around his eyes, and then he was as blind as a bat.

"Now," said the old man, "throw your leg over what you feel and hold fast."

The fisherman reached down his hand, and there felt the back of something rough and hairy. He flung his leg over it, and—Whisk! Whizz! Off he shot through the air like a sky-rocket. Nothing was left for him to do but grip tightly with hands and feet and to hold fast. On they went, and on they went, until, after a great while, whatever it was that was carrying him lit upon the ground, and there the fisherman found himself standing, for that which had brought him had gone.

The old man whipped the handkerchief off his eyes, and there the fisherman found himself on the shores of the sea, where there was nothing to be seen but water upon one side and rocks and naked sand upon the other.

"This is the place for you to cast your nets," said the old magician; "for if we catch nothing here we catch nothing at all."

The fisherman unrolled his nets and cast them and dragged them, and then cast them and dragged them again, but neither time caught so much as a herring. But the third time that he cast he found that he had caught something that weighed as heavy as lead. He pulled and pulled, until by-and-by he dragged the load ashore, and what should it be but a great chest of wood, blackened by the sea-water, and covered with shells and green moss.

That was the very thing that the magician had come to fish for.

From his pouch the old man took a little golden key, which he fitted into a key-hole in the side of the chest. He threw back the lid; the fisherman looked within, and there was the prettiest little palace that man's eye ever beheld, all made of mother-of-pearl and silver-frosted as white as snow. The old magician lifted the little palace out of the box and set it upon the ground.

Then, lo and behold! A marvelous thing happened; for the palace instantly began to grow for all the world like a soap-bubble, until it stood in the moonlight gleaming and glistening like snow, the windows bright with the lights of a thousand wax tapers, and the sound of music and voices and laughter coming from within.

Hardly could the fisherman catch his breath from one strange thing when another happened. The old magician took off his clothes and his face—yes, his face—for all the world as though it had been a mask, and there stood as handsome and noble a young man as ever the light looked on. Then, beckoning to the fisherman, dumb with wonder, he led the way up the great flight of marble steps to the palace door. As he came the door swung open with a blaze of light, and there stood hundreds of noblemen, all clad in silks and satins and velvets, who, when they saw the magician, bowed low before him, as though he had been a king. Leading the way, they brought the two through halls and chambers and room after room, each more magnificent than the other, until they came to one that surpassed a hundredfold any of the others.

At the farther end was a golden throne, and upon it sat a lady more lovely and beautiful than a dream, her eyes as bright as diamonds, her cheeks like rose leaves, and her hair like spun gold. She came half-way down the steps of the throne to welcome the magician, and when the two met they kissed one another before all those who were looking on. Then she brought him to the throne and seated him beside her, and there they talked for a long time very earnestly.

Nobody said a word to the fisherman, who stood staring about him like an owl. "I wonder," said he to himself at last, "if they will give a body a bite to eat by-and-by?" For, to tell the truth, the good supper that he had come away from at home had left a sharp hunger gnawing at his insides, and he longed for something good and warm to fill the empty place. But time passed, and not so much as a crust of bread was brought to stay his stomach.

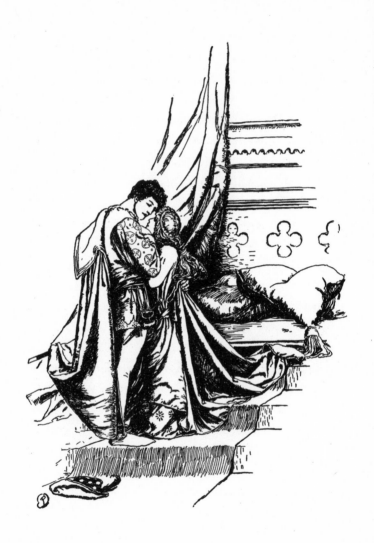

By-and-by the clock struck twelve, and then the two who sat upon the throne arose. The beautiful lady took the magician by the hand, and, turning to those who stood around, said, in a loud voice, "Behold him who alone is worthy to possess the jewel of jewels! Unto him do I give it, and with it all power of powers!" Thereon she opened a golden casket that stood beside her, and brought thence a little crystal ball, about as big as a pigeon's egg, in which was something that glistened like a spark of fire. The magician took the crystal ball and thrust it into his bosom; but what it was the fisherman could not guess, and if you do not know I shall not tell you.

Then for the first time the beautiful lady seemed to notice the fisherman. She beckoned him, and when he stood beside her two men came carrying a chest. The chief treasurer opened it, and it was full of bags of gold money. "How will you have it?" said the beautiful lady.

"Have what?" said the fisherman.

"Have the pay for your labor?" said the beautiful lady.

"I will," said the fisherman, promptly, "take it in my hat."

"So be it," said the beautiful lady. She waved her hand, and the chief treasurer took a bag from the chest, untied it, and emptied a cataract of gold into the fur cap. The fisherman had never seen so much wealth in all his life before, and he stood like a man turned to stone.

"Is all this mine?" said the fisherman.

"It is," said the beautiful lady.

"Then God bless your pretty eyes," said the fisherman.

Then the magician kissed the beautiful lady, and, beckoning to the fisherman, left the throne-room the same way that they had come. The noblemen, in silks and satins and velvets, marched ahead, and back they went through the other apartments, until at last they came to the door.

Out they stepped, and then what do you suppose happened?

If the wonderful palace had grown like a bubble, like a bubble it vanished. There the two stood on the sea-shore, with nothing to be seen but rocks and sand and water, and the starry sky overhead.

The fisherman shook his cap of gold, and it jingled and tinkled, and was as heavy as lead. If it was not all a dream, he was rich for life. "But anyhow," said he, "they might have given a body a bite to eat."

The magician put on his red clothes and his face again, making himself as hoary and as old as before. He took out his flint and steel, and his sticks of spice-wood and his gray powder, and made a great fire and smoke just as he had done before. Then again he tied his handkerchief over the fisherman's eyes. "Remember," said he, "what I told you when we started upon our journey. Keep your mouth tight shut, for if you utter so much as a single word you are a lost man. Now throw your leg over what you feel and hold fast."

The fisherman had his net over one arm and his cap of gold in the other hand; nevertheless, there he felt the same hairy thing he had felt before. He flung his leg over it, and away he was gone through the air like a sky-rocket.

Now, he had grown somewhat used to strange things by this time, so he began to think that he would like to see what sort of a creature it was upon which he was riding thus through the sky. So he contrived, in spite of his net and cap, to push up the handkerchief from over one eye. Out he peeped, and then he saw as clear as day what the strange steed was.

He was riding upon a he-goat as black as night, and in front of him was the magician riding upon just such another, his great red robe fluttering out behind him in the moonlight like huge red wings.

"Great herring and little fishes!" roared the fisherman; "it is a billy-goat!"

Instantly goats, old man, and all were gone like a flash. Down fell the fisherman through the empty sky, whirling over and over and around and around like a frog. He held tightly to his net, but away flew his fur cap, the golden money falling in a shower like sparks of yellow light. Down he fell and down he fell, until his head spun like a top.

By good-luck his house was just below, with its thatch of soft rushes. Into the very middle of it he tumbled, and right through the thatch—bump!—into the room below.

The good wife was in bed, snoring away for dear life; but such a noise as the fisherman made coming into the house was enough to wake the dead. Up she jumped, and there she sat, staring and winking with sleep, and with her brains as addled as a duck's egg in a thunder-storm.

"There!" said the fisherman, as he gathered himself up and rubbed his shoulder, "that is what comes of following a woman's advice!"

"WHOSE turn is it next?" said Dr. Faustus, lighting a fresh pipe of tobacco.

"'Tis the turn of yonder old gentleman," said the Soldier who cheated the Devil, and he pointed with the stem of his pipe to the Fisherman who unbottled the Genie that King Solomon had corked and thrown into the sea. "Every one else has told a story, and now it is his turn."

"I will not deny, my friend, that what you say is true, and that it is my turn," said the Fisherman. "Nor will I deny that I have already a story in my mind. It is," said he, "about a certain prince, and of how he went through many and one adventures, and at last discovered that which is—

16

THE SALT OF LIFE

Once upon a time there was a king who had three sons, and by the time that the youngest prince had down upon his chin the king had grown so old that the cares of the kingdom began to rest over heavily upon his shoulders. So he called his chief councilor and told him that he was of a mind to let the princes reign in his stead. To the son who loved him the best he would give the largest part of his kingdom, to the son who loved him the next best the next part, and to the son who loved him the least the least part. The old councilor was very wise and shook his head, but the king's mind had long been settled as to what he was about to do. So he called the princes to him one by one and asked each as to how much he loved him.

"I love you as a mountain of gold," said the oldest prince,

and the king was very pleased that his son should give him such love.

"I love you as a mountain of silver," said the second prince, and the king was pleased with that also.

But when the youngest prince was called, he did not answer at first, but thought and thought. At last he looked up. "I love you," said he, "as I love salt."

When the king heard what his youngest son said he was filled with anger. "What!" he cried, "do you love me no better than salt—a stuff that is the most bitter of all things to the taste, and the cheapest and the commonest of all things in the world? Away with you, and never let me see your face again! Henceforth you are no son of mine."

The prince would have spoken, but the king would not allow him, and bade his guards thrust the young man forth from the room.

Now the queen loved the youngest prince the best of all her sons, and when she heard how the king was about to drive him forth into the wide world to shift for himself, she wept and wept. "Ah, my son!" said she to him, "it is little or nothing that I have to give you. Nevertheless, I have one precious thing. Here is a ring; take it and wear it always, for so long as you have it upon your finger no magic can have power over you."

Thus it was that the youngest prince set forth into the wide world with little or nothing but a ring upon his finger.

For seven days he traveled on, and knew not where he was going or whither his footsteps led. At the end of that time he came to the gates of a town. The prince entered the gates, and found himself in a city the like of which he had never seen in his life before for grandeur and magnificence—beautiful palaces and gardens, stores and bazaars crowded with rich stuffs of satin and silk and wrought silver and gold of cunning workmanship; for the land to which he had come was the richest in all of the world. All that day he wandered up and down, and thought nothing of weariness and hunger for wonder of all that he saw. But at last evening drew down, and he began to bethink himself of somewhere to lodge during the night.

Just then he came to a bridge, over the wall of which leaned an old man with a long white beard, looking down into the water. He was dressed richly but soberly, and every now and then he sighed and groaned, and as the prince drew near he saw the tears falling—drip, drip—from the old man's eyes.

The prince had a kind heart, and could not bear to see one in distress; so he spoke to the old man, and asked him his trouble.

"Ah, me!" said the other, "only yesterday I had a son, tall and handsome like yourself. But the queen took him to sup with her, and I am left all alone in my old age, like a tree stripped of leaves and fruit."

"But surely," said the prince, "it can be no such sad matter to sup with a queen. That is an honor that most men covet."

"Ah!" said the old man, "you are a stranger in this place, or else you would know that no youth so chosen to sup with the queen ever returns to his home again."

"Yes," said the prince, "I am a stranger and have only come hither this day, and so do not understand these things. Even when I found you I was about to ask the way to some inn where folk of good condition lodge."

"Then come home with me tonight," said the old man. "I live all alone, and I will tell you the trouble that lies upon this country." Thereupon, taking the prince by the arm, he led him across the bridge and to another quarter of the town where he dwelt. He bade the servants prepare a fine supper, and he and the prince sat down to the table together. After they had made an end of eating and drinking, the old man told the prince all concerning those things of which he had spoken, and thus it was:

"When the king of this land died he left behind him three daughters—the most beautiful princesses in all of the world.

"Folk hardly dared speak of the eldest of them, but

whisperings said that she was a sorceress, and that strange and gruesome things were done by her. The second princess was also a witch, though it was not said that she was evil, like the other. As for the youngest of the three, she was as beautiful as the morning and as gentle as a dove. When she was born a golden thread was about her neck, and it was foretold of her that she was to be the queen of the land.

"But not long after the old king died the youngest princess vanished—no one could tell whither, and no one dared to ask—and the eldest princess had herself crowned as queen, and no one dared gainsay her. For a while everything went well enough, but by-and-by evil days came upon the land. Once every seven days the queen would bid some youth, young and strong, to sup with her, and from that time no one ever heard of him again, and no one dared ask what had become of him. At first it was the great folk at the queen's palace—officers and courtiers—who suffered; but by-and-by the sons of the merchants and the chief men of the city began to be taken. One time," said the old man, "I myself had three sons—as noble young men as could be found in the wide world. One day the chief of the queen's officers came to my house and asked me concerning how many sons I had. I was forced to tell him, and in a little while they were taken one by one to the queen's palace, and I never saw them again.

"But misfortune, like death, comes upon the young as well as the old. You yourself have had trouble, or else I am mistaken. Tell me what lies upon your heart, my son, for the talking of it makes the burthen lighter."

The prince did as the old man bade him, and told all of his story; and so they sat talking and talking until far into the night, and the old man grew fonder and fonder of the prince the more he saw of him. So the end of the matter was that he asked the prince to live with him as his son, seeing that the young man had now no father and he no children, and the prince consented gladly enough.

So the two lived together like father and son, and the good old man began to take some joy in life once more.

But one day who should come riding up to the door but the chief of the queen's officers.

"How is this?" said he to the old man, when he saw the prince. "Did you not tell me that you had but three sons, and is this not a fourth?"

It was of no use for the old man to tell the officer that the youth was not his son, but was a prince who had come to visit that country. The officer drew forth his tablets and wrote something upon them, and then went his way, leaving the old man sighing and groaning. "Ah, me!" said he, "my heart sadly forebodes trouble."

Sure enough, before three days had passed a bidding came to the prince to make ready to sup with the queen that night.

When evening drew near a troop of horsemen came, bringing a white horse with a saddle and bridle of gold studded with precious stones, to take the prince to the queen's palace.

As soon as they had brought him thither they led the prince to a room where was a golden table spread with a snow-white cloth and set with dishes of gold. At the end of the table the queen sat waiting for him, and her face was hidden by a veil of silver gauze. She raised the veil and looked at the prince, and when he saw her face he stood as one wonder-struck, for not only was she so beautiful, but she set a spell upon him with the evil charm of her eyes. No one sat at the table but the queen and the prince, and a score of young pages served them, and sweet music sounded from a curtained gallery.

At last came midnight, and suddenly a great gong sounded from the court-yard outside. Then in an instant the music was stopped, the pages that served them hurried from the room, and presently all was as still as death.

Then, when all were gone, the queen arose and beckoned the prince, and he had no choice but to arise also and follow whither she led. She took him through the palace, where all was as still as the grave, and so came out by a postern door into a garden. Beside the postern a torch burned in a bracket. The queen took it down, and then led the prince up a path and under the silent trees until they came to a great wall of rough stone. She pressed her hand upon one of the great stones, and it opened like a door, and there was a flight of steps that led downward. The queen descended these steps, and the prince followed closely behind her. At the bottom was a long passage-way, and at the farther end the prince saw what looked like a bright spark of light, as though the sun were shining. She thrust the torch into another bracket in the wall of the passage, and then led the way towards the light. It grew larger and larger as they went forward, until at last they came out at the farther end, and there the prince found himself standing in the sunlight and not far from the seashore. The queen led the way towards the shore, when suddenly a great number of black dogs came running towards them, barking and snarling, and showing their teeth as though they would tear the two in pieces. But the queen drew from her bosom a whip with a steel-pointed lash, and as the dogs came springing towards them she laid about her right and left, till the skin flew and the blood ran, and the dogs leaped away howling and yelping.

At the edge of the water was a great stone mill, and the queen pointed towards it and bade the prince turn it. Strong as he was, it was as much as he could do to work it; but grind it he did, though the sweat ran down his face in streams. By-and-by a speck appeared far away upon the water; and as the prince ground and ground at the mill the speck grew larger and larger. It was something upon the water, and it came nearer and nearer as swiftly as the wind. At last it came close enough for him to see that it was a little boat all of brass. By-and-by the boat struck upon the beach, and as soon as it did so the queen entered it, bidding the prince do the same.

No sooner were they seated than away the boat went, still as swiftly as the wind. On it flew and on it flew, until at last they came to another shore, the like of which the prince had never seen in his life before. Down to the edge of the water ran a garden—but such a garden! The leaves of the trees were all of silver and the fruit of gold, and instead of flowers were precious stones—white, red, yellow, blue, and green—that flashed like sparks of sunlight as the breeze moved them this way and that way. Beyond the silver trees, with their golden fruit, was a great palace as white as snow, and so bright that one had to shut one's eyes as one looked upon it.

The boat ran up on the beach close to just such a stone mill as the prince had seen upon the other side of the water, and then he and the queen stepped ashore. As soon as they had done so the brazen boat floated swiftly away, and in a little while was gone.

"Here our journey ends," said the queen. "Is it not a wonderful land, and well worth the seeing? Look at all these jewels and this gold, as plenty as fruits and flowers at home. You may take what you please; but while you are gathering them I have another matter after which I must look. Wait for me here, and by-and-by I will be back again."

So saying, she turned and left the prince, going towards the castle back of the trees.

But the prince was a prince, and not a common man; he cared nothing for gold and jewels. What he did care for was to see where the queen went, and why she had brought him to this strange land. So, as soon as she had fairly gone, he followed after.

He went along under the gold and silver trees, in the direction she had taken, until at last he came to a tall flight of steps that led up to the doorway of the snow-white palace. The door stood open, and into it the prince went. He saw not a soul, but he heard a noise as of blows and the sound as of some one weeping. He followed the sound, until by-and-by he came to a great vaulted room in the very center of the palace. A curtain hung at the doorway. The prince lifted it and peeped within, and this was what he saw:

In the middle of the room was a marble basin of water as clear as crystal, and around the sides of the basin were these words, written in letters of gold:

"Whatsoever is False, that I make True."

Beside the fountain upon a marble stand stood a statue of a beautiful woman made of alabaster, and around the neck of the statue was a thread of gold. The queen stood beside the statue, and beat and beat it with her steel-tipped whip. And all the while she lashed it the statue sighed and groaned like a living being, and the tears ran down its stone cheeks as though it were suffering. By-and-by the queen rested for a moment, and said, panting, "Will you give me the thread of gold?" and the statue answered "No." Whereupon she fell to raining blows upon it as she had done before.

So she continued, now beating the statue and now asking it whether it would give her the thread of gold, to which the statue always answered "No," and all the while the prince stood gazing and wondering. By-and-by the queen wearied of what she was doing, and thrust the steel-tipped lash back into her bosom again, upon which the prince, seeing that she was done, hurried back to the garden where she had left him and pretended to be gathering the golden fruit and jewel flowers.

The queen said nothing to him good or bad, except to command him to grind at the great stone mill as he had done on the other side of the water. Thereupon the prince did as she bade, and presently the brazen boat came skimming over the water more swiftly than the wind. Again the queen and the prince entered it, and again it carried them to the other side whence they had come.

No sooner had the queen set foot upon the shore than she stooped and gathered up a handful of sand. Then, turning as quick as lightning, she flung it into the prince's face. "Be a black dog," she cried in a loud voice, "and join your comrades!"

And now it was that the ring that the prince's mother had given him stood him in good stead. But for it he would have become a black dog like those others, for thus it had happened to all before him who had ferried the witch queen over the water. So she expected to see him run away yelping, as those others had done; but the prince remained a prince, and stood looking her in the face.

When the queen saw that her magic had failed her she grew as pale as death, and fell to trembling in every limb. She turned and hastened quickly away, and the prince followed her wondering, for he neither knew the mischief she had intended doing him, nor how his ring had saved him from the fate of those others.

So they came back up the stairs and out through the stone wall into the palace garden. The queen pressed her hand against the stone and it turned back into its place again. Then, beckoning to the prince, she hurried away down the garden.

Before he followed he picked up a coal that lay near by, and put a cross upon the stone; then he hurried after her, and so came to the palace once more.

By this time the cocks were crowing, and the dawn of day was just beginning to show over the roof-tops and the chimney-stacks of the town.

As for the queen, she had regained her composure, and, bidding the prince wait for her a moment, she hastened to her chamber. There she opened her book of magic, and in it she soon found who the prince was and how the ring had saved him.

When she had learned all that she wanted to know she put on a smiling face and came back to him. "Ah, prince," said she, "I well know who you are, for your coming to my country is no secret to me. I have shown you strange things tonight. I will unfold all the wonder to you another time. Will you not come back and sup with me again?"

"Yes," said the prince, "I will come whensoever you bid me;" for he was curious to know the secret of the statue and the strange things he had seen.

"And will you not give me a pledge of your coming?" said the queen, still smiling.

"What pledge shall I give you?" asked the prince.

"Give me the ring that is upon your finger," said the queen;

and she smiled so bewitchingly that the prince could not have refused her had he desired to do so.

Alas for him! He thought no evil, but, without a word, drew off the ring and gave it to the queen, and she slipped it upon her finger.

"O fool!" she cried, laughing a wicked laugh, "O fool! To give away that in which your safety lay!" As she spoke she dipped her fingers into a basin of water that stood near by and dashed the drops into the prince's face. "Be a raven," she cried, "and a raven remain!"

In an instant the prince was a prince no longer, but a coal-black raven. The queen snatched up a sword that lay near by and struck at him to kill him. But the raven-prince leaped aside and the blow missed its aim.

By good luck a window stood open, and before the queen could strike again he spread his wings and flew out of the open casement and over the house-tops, and was gone.

On he flew and on he flew until he came to the old man's house, and so to the room where his foster-father himself was sitting. He lit upon the ground at the old man's feet and tried to tell him what had befallen, but all that he could say was "Croak! croak!"

"What brings this bird of ill omen?" said the old man, and

he drew his sword to kill it. He raised his hand to strike, but the raven did not try to fly away as he had expected, but bowed his neck to receive the stroke. Then the old man saw that the tears were running down from the raven's eyes, and he held his hand. "What strange thing is this?" he said. "Surely nothing but the living soul weeps; and how, then, can this bird shed tears?" So he took the raven up and looked into his eyes, and in them he saw the prince's soul. "Alas!" he cried, "my heart misgives me that something strange has happened. Tell me, is this not my foster-son, the prince?"

The raven answered "Croak!" and nothing else, but the good old man understood it all, and the tears ran down his cheeks and trickled over his beard. "Whether man or raven, you shall still be my son," said he, and he held the raven close in his arms and caressed it.

He had a golden cage made for the bird, and every day he would walk with it in the garden, talking to it as a father talks to his son.

One day when they were thus in the garden together a strange lady came towards them down the pathway. Over her head and face was drawn a thick veil, so that the two could not tell who she was. When she came close to them she raised the veil, and the raven-prince saw that her face was the living

329

likeness of the queen's; and yet there was something in it that was different. It was the second sister of the queen, and the old man knew her and bowed before her.

"Listen," said she. "I know what the raven is, and that it is the prince, whom the queen has bewitched. I also know nearly as much of magic as she, and it is that alone that has saved me so long from ill. But danger hangs close over me; the queen only waits for the chance to bewitch me; and some day she will overpower me, for she is stronger than I. With the prince's aid I can overcome her and make myself forever safe, and it is this that has brought me here today. My magic is powerful enough to change the prince back into his true shape again, and I will do so if he will aid me in what follows, and this is it: I will conjure the queen, and by-and-by a great eagle will come flying, and its plumage will be as black as night. Then I myself will become an eagle, with black-and-white plumage, and we two will fight in the air. After a while we will both fall to the ground, and then the prince must cut off the head of the black eagle with a knife I shall give him. Will you do this," said she, turning to the raven, "if I transform you to your true shape?"

The raven bowed his head and said "Croak!" And the sister of the queen knew that he meant yes.

Therewith she drew a great, long, keen knife from her

bosom, and thrust it into the ground. "It is with this knife of magic," said she, "that you must cut off the black eagle's head." Then the witch-princess gathered up some sand in her hand, and flung it into the raven's face. "Resume," cried she, "your own shape!" And in an instant the prince was himself again. The next thing the sister of the queen did was to draw a circle upon the ground around the prince, the old man, and herself. On the circle she marked strange figures here and there. Then, all three standing close together, she began her conjurations, uttering strange words—now under her breath, and now clear and loud.

Presently the sky darkened, and it began to thunder and rumble. Darker it grew and darker, and the thunder crashed and roared. The earth trembled under their feet, and the trees swayed hither and thither as though tossed by a tempest. Then suddenly the uproar ceased and all grew as still as death, the clouds rolled away, and in a moment the sun shone out once more, and all was calm and serene as it had been before. But still the princess muttered her conjurations, and as the prince and the old man looked they beheld a speck that grew larger and larger, until they saw that it was an eagle as black as night that was coming swiftly flying through the sky. Then the queen's sister also saw it and ceased from her spells. She drew a little cap of feathers from her bosom with trembling hands.

"Remember," said she to the prince; and, so saying, clapped the feather cap upon her head. In an instant she herself became an eagle—pied, black and white—and, spreading her wings, leaped into the air.

For a while the two eagles circled around and around; but at last they dashed against one another, and, grappling with their talons, tumbled over and over until they struck the ground close to the two who stood looking.

Then the prince snatched the knife from the ground and ran to where they lay struggling. "Which was I to kill?" said he to the old man.

"Are they not birds of a feather?" cried the foster-father. "Kill them both, for then only shall we all be safe."

The prince needed no second telling to see the wisdom of what the old man said. In an instant he struck off the heads of both the eagles, and thus put an end to both sorceresses, the lesser as well as the greater. They buried both of the eagles in the garden without telling any one of what had happened. So soon as that was done the old man bade the prince tell him all that had befallen him, and the prince did so.

"Aye! Aye!" said the old man, "I see it all as clear as day. The black dogs are the young men who have supped with the queen; the statue is the good princess; and the basin of water is the water of life, which has the power of taking away magic.

Come; let us make haste to bring help to all those poor unfortunates who have been lying under the queen's spells."

The prince needed no urging to do that. They hurried to the palace; they crossed the garden to the stone wall. There they found the stone upon which the prince had set the black cross. He pressed his hand upon it, and it opened to him like a door. They descended the steps, and went through the passageway, until they came out upon the sea-shore. The black dogs came leaping towards them; but this time it was to fawn upon them, and to lick their hands and faces.

The prince turned the great stone mill till the brazen boat came flying towards the shore. They entered it, and so crossed the water and came to the other side. They did not tarry in the garden, but went straight to the snow-white palace and to the great vaulted chamber where was the statue. "Yes," said the old man, "it is the youngest princess, sure enough."

The prince said nothing, but he dipped up some of the water in his palm and dashed it upon the statue. "If you are the princess, take your true shape again," said he. Before the words had left his lips the statue became flesh and blood, and the princess stepped down from where she stood, and the prince thought that he had never seen any one so beautiful as she. "You have brought me back to life," said she, "and whatever I shall have shall be yours as well as mine."

Then they all set their faces homeward again, and the prince took with him a cupful of the water of life.

When they reached the farther shore the black dogs came running to meet them. The prince sprinkled the water he carried upon them, and as soon as it touched them that instant they were black dogs no longer, but the tall, noble young men that the sorceress queen had bewitched. There, as the old man had hoped, he found his own three sons, and kissed them with the tears running down his face.

But when the people of that land learned that their youngest princess, and the one whom they loved, had come back again, and that the two sorceresses would trouble them no longer, they shouted and shouted for joy. All the town was hung with flags and illuminated, the fountains ran with wine, and nothing was heard but sounds of rejoicing. In the midst of it all the prince married the princess, and so became the king of that country.

And now to go back again to the beginning.

After the youngest prince had been driven away from home, and the old king had divided the kingdom betwixt the other two, things went for a while smoothly and joyfully. But by little and little the king was put to one side until he became as nothing in his own land. At last hot words passed between the father and the two sons, and the end of the matter was that the king was driven from the land to shift for himself.

Now, after the youngest prince had married and had become king of that other land, he bethought himself of his father and his mother, and longed to see them again. So he set forth and traveled towards his old home. In his journeying he came to a lonely house at the edge of a great forest, and there night came upon him. He sent one of the many of those who rode with him to ask whether he could not find lodging there for the time, and who should answer the summons but the king, his father, dressed in the coarse clothing of a forester. The old king did not know his own son in the kingly young king who sat upon his snow-white horse. He bade the visitor to enter, and he and the old queen served their son and bowed before him.

The next morning the young king rode back to his own land, and then sent attendants with horses and splendid clothes, and bade them bring his father and mother to his own home.

He had a noble feast set for them, with everything befitting the entertainment of a king, but he ordered that not a grain of salt should season it.

So the father and the mother sat down to the feast with

their son and his queen, but all the time they did not know him. The old king tasted the food and tasted the food, but he could not eat of it.

"Do you not feel hungry?" said the young king.

"Alas," said his father, "I crave your majesty's pardon, but there is no salt in the food."

"And so is life lacking of savor without love," said the young king; "and yet because I loved you as salt you disowned me and cast me out into the world."

Therewith he could contain himself no longer, but with the tears running down his cheeks kissed his father and his mother; and they knew him, and kissed him again.

Afterwards the young king went with a great army into the country of his elder brothers, and, overcoming them, set his father upon his throne again. If ever the two got back their crowns you may be sure that they wore them more modestly than they did the first time.

SO the Fisherman who had one time unbottled the Genie whom Solomon the Wise had stoppered up concluded his story, and all of the good folk who were there began clapping their shadowy hands.

"Aye, aye," said old Bidpai, "there is much truth in what you say, for it is verily so that that which men—call—love—is—the—salt—of—"

His voice had been fading away thinner and thinner and smaller and smaller—now it was like the shadow of a voice; now it trembled and quivered out into silence and was gone.

And with the voice of old Bidpai the pleasant Land of Twilight was also gone. As a breath fades away from a mirror, so had it faded and vanished into nothingness.

I opened my eyes.

There was a yellow light—it came from the evening lamp. There were people of flesh and blood around—my own dear people—and they were talking together. There was the library with the rows of books looking silently on from their shelves. There was the fire of hickory logs crackling and snapping in the fireplace, and throwing a wavering, yellow light on the wall.

Had I been asleep? No; I had been in Twilight Land.

And now the pleasant Twilight Land had gone. It had faded out, and I was back again in the work-a-day world.

There I was sitting in my chair; and, what was more, it was time for the children to go to bed.

ABOUT THE AUTHOR

Howard Pyle (1853–1911) was an American author, illustrator, and teacher who inspired a generation of artists, from N. C. Wyeth to Jessie Wilcox Smith. Born in Wilmington, Delaware, Pyle spent his early years immersed in such stories as the Grimm Brothers' tales and the Arabian Nights. After studying art in Philadelphia, he set up a small studio and began a long and successful career as a writer and illustrator. He taught at Philadelphia's Drexel Institute of Art, Science, and Industry before opening the Howard Pyle School of Art in 1900. He is best known for *The Merry Adventures of Robin Hood,* a compilation of Robin Hood legends adapted for children.

ABOUT LOOKING GLASS LIBRARY

The Looking Glass Library series features the world's finest fairy tales, adventure stories, and fantasy novels—yesterday's classics for today's readers.